THE RAVEN
EPISODE I-III

ORIGINS - FREEDOM - THE RIPPER

TOBEY ALEXANDER

TAGS CREATIVE

Recite the prophecy, respect it's promise.

A burnt jewel,

A hell demons throne,

Both twins will meet a fight.

The Full Moon Society will greet them all in victory.

EPISODE

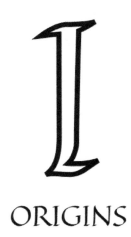

ORIGINS

1

FATED MEETINGS

NUTHALL SECURE HOSPITAL, LONDON

K imberley Mansfield was worried. Despite her outward appearance, she hugged the pile of files and paperwork to her chest as she followed the gruff orderly along the corridors of the hospital. It had taken her almost seven months of back and forth to convince the warden to allow her access to the prisoners as part of her thesis. That and the conversations with the ethics board had almost made her give in, but the cajoling from her tutor had kept the spark alive.

Now, as she walked along the sterile corridors, it suddenly felt worth the effort.

'You're one of the first to be allowed in here. Must have impressed the warden or something. She's not usually one for allowing other people in here.'

'I guess I'm, well, lucky?' Her nervousness was showing, and she silently berated herself as she moved to join the orderly.

'I'd hardly call it lucky!'

The orderly was in his early thirties, weathered and grumpy. His jet-black hair was swept back, and he had a cold unkindness to his facade. Kimberley was not unfamiliar with the type of people that worked in places such as the Nuthall. There had to be an air of disconnect from the patients, and this man was no exception. Watching his expression, they reached a secure door at the end of the corridor and the orderly set about presenting his ID card towards the reader.

'What do you mean by that?'

'This place isn't exactly the sort of place young girls should come,' he offered as the door unlocked and he pulled it open. 'Patients here haven't seen anyone but the staff for some time. I expect a pretty little thing like you might stir some attention.'

'Spare me the Silence Of The Lambs routine, but this isn't my first visit to a place like this.'

'Oh, I think you'll find it is.'

There was something about the orderly's smirk that begged for further interrogation, but Kimberley was cut short as they arrived at a second security station. Ignoring the conversations between the orderly and the security staff, Kimberley moved to the wide window that looked out into the main atrium of the hospital site.

It wasn't what she had been expecting in the slightest. The streamline and sterile modern interior was at odds with the normal dingy appearance she had become accustomed to. Often the places they gave her access to had occupied some aged historical building, but this, this was something different. Looking down, she realised they were three levels above the ground, with levels of secure accommodation and sectioned areas for so-called free movement.

'It's different from what I'm used to,' Kimberley remarked as the orderly joined her and thrust out an identification badge marked VISITOR into her hand. 'It's a lot cleaner.'

'We aren't completely government funded. We have the luxury of being sponsored by a variety of outside sources.'

'I thought you weren't a private facility.'

'We sit on that fine line between public and private. The warden's done well to get us what we need and keep us ticking over as we do.'

'Looks like she's doing a good job.' Kimberley sensed there was more to what the man was saying, but thought better than to press. 'Will I get to meet her when I'm done?'

'We'll have to see what her schedule looks like, but she is keen to put a face to the name.' Stepping back from the window, he looked at the security staff, who offered a curt nod. 'Shall we?'

'Who am I being given access to?'

'Ah yes, how remiss of me.' Stepping back to the security booth, the orderly picked up a paper file and handed it to Kimberley. 'The warden has selected patients based on the profile questionnaire you sent. You'll be meeting John Smith.'

'John Smith?'

'While he's brought up from *The Deck*, you'll have time to go over his paperwork.'

'I'm surprised it's not on a USB or something,' Kimberley replied as she precariously held onto the paperwork and tried to peek inside the file.

'Technology has its place, but good old paper can't be copied or taken away. You'll have to surrender that when you're done.'

'Can I make notes?'

'Yes.'

Opening the next set of doors, Kimberley followed on in silence and slipped the manilla folder into the pile of paperwork she had brought with her. After what felt like an age of security doors and airlock style thoroughfares, Kimberley found herself in a narrow glass lift that descended towards what the orderly had called *The Deck*.

'How many patients are there?'

'Last count, just over two-hundred.'

'It's a big facility for such a small number.'

'Trust me,' the orderly scoffed as the lift ground to a halt. 'That's capacity, especially considering how much help some of them need.'

On cue, the lift doors opened, and the air was filled with the chatter of voices and sounds of muffled screams. Kimberley was familiar with the sounds of places like this and while the sterile exterior attempted to portray a different story, the sounds echoing in the vast open space told her it was just the same as all the others she had visited.

'You can take a seat in there. It'll be about twenty-minutes until he's ready.'

'Can I see him in his everyday surrounding before I meet him?'

Pausing at the door to a small holding room, the orderly stopped short of opening it. Turning to face her, Kimberley suddenly felt small in his shadow as his gaze bore into her.

'Like I said up there, you're not here to upset the balance. The fewer patients that see you the better.' Pushing open the door, he indicated for her to enter. 'That's why you'll be interviewing him in the old wing.'

'Old wing?'

'More like what you're used to visiting. Now, if you don't mind.'

Not giving her any chance to reply, the orderly stepped back over the threshold and pulled the door shut behind him. Dropping her paperwork onto a small coffee table, Kimberley spied the coffee machine in the corner and quickly made herself as comfortable as she could.

Having poured a mug of what would undoubtedly be stale-tasting coffee, she moved back to the table and dropped into the plastic chair to scour through the folder they had given her. Unsurprisingly, the contents were light. The pages that had been collated were out of order and immediately she noticed from the first three pages, the numbering in the top right corner skipped from single figures to the high forties.

'Seems there's a lot they don't want me to know about you, John Smith.' Kimberley hushed as she flipped open her notepad and set about making her notes.

Lost in the file, Kimberley jumped in her seat when the orderly pushed open the door. Casting a glance at her watch, it surprised her to see almost an hour had passed since she had fetched the now lukewarm coffee from the machine and set about making her notes.

'He's ready for you.'

'Just let me sort my stuff out.'

The orderly loitered at the threshold to the small waiting room as Kimberley hurried to pile her paperwork together. As she scooped it back into her arms, the gentle flickering of a red light in the room's corner caught her attention. Mounted in the shadows, she noticed a small CCTV camera pointing directly down at where she had been sitting. Although it was not an unfamiliar sight in a secure hospital, the fact she hadn't realised she was being watched made her feel uneasy.

'It's only a couple minutes' walk from here and then you've got the rest of the morning with him. We break for lunch at half-past one.'

'And do I get to continue after lunch?'

'Yes. You'll have until three o'clock.'

'Thank you.'

Passing through a curious set of doors, Kimberley found herself once again in more familiar surroundings. Unlike the sleek lines of the main building, she now found herself in the tighter confines of a Victorian brick building. Immediately, the air changed from cool air-conditioned to damp and stale. This was more what she had become accustomed to during her dissertation research, and she once again felt at home as they descended a spiral staircase and found themselves in a narrow corridor. Imposing metal doors lined one side, while the other was plain brick with no doors or windows.

'This one's yours.' The orderly snapped as they reached the third rusted door along. 'I'll be down there watching on the cameras.'

'Ok.' Kimberley fought to hide her nerves.

'Please remember the paperwork you signed coming in. No digital recording devices other than cassette tapes and paper notes.'

'I remember.'

'Oh, and one last thing.' The orderly added as he slipped the key into the oversized lock. 'No touching.'

'Touching?'

'Keep your hands to yourself. Keep your distance from him and you'll be fine.'

'Why, is he dangerous?' Kimberley's heart pounded in her ears. 'There weren't any warning markers on the front sheet of his file.'

'Just trust me.'

Pulling open the door, Kimberley's attention turned into the small interview cell and what waited for her inside.

Silently scorning herself, Kimberley couldn't help but smile at her own foolishness. The orderly had done a very good job of getting her mind racing as they had made their way into the depths of the hospital. Seeing John Smith shackled to the table in the centre of the room, she was reminded how playful the staff could be. Walking into the room, she shrugged off the idiotic concern she had allowed to grow in her stomach and waited for the door to close.

'I must be doing something right. The warden never lets me have visitors.'

John Smith looked normal. Nothing about his exterior betrayed any of the ailments that had been noted in his file. Apart from looking in need of a good meal and a shave, there was something almost handsome about his appearance as he sat dressed in the drab grey clothes the hospital had issued him. Behind the blonde fringe that danced over his forehead, Kimberley could see his strikingly blue eyes as they looked up at her from across the table. John looked to be in his early thirties, but his eyes and the dark circles around them told a different story.

'Did they tell you who I am and why I'm here?'

'You're a student, doing research on long-term patients detained in the public healthcare system.'

'Something like that.'

'Please, take a seat.'

Accepting the offer, Kimberley lowered her papers onto the table and set about making the space her own on the table. Feeling his eyes on her, Kimberley chanced a glance and was surprised to see an amused smile on his face.

'Something amusing you?'

'Nothing.' John smirked and leant back in his chair. 'I was admiring your clothes.'

'I beg your pardon.'

'They're different from what I remember. All I see are white uniforms or grey ones.'

'How long have you been here?'

'Doesn't it say in that little file they've given you?'

'Actually, no.' Kimberley had noticed a lot of the relevant dates had been missing from the summary.

'That's not surprising. I can't imagine they'd want you knowing everything.'

'Well, why don't you tell me what you think I want to know.'

'Get yourself settled first. I expect you'll need to start that thing recording before we get started. I'd hate for you to miss any of the finer details.'

Kimberley felt like John was playing with her. Having experienced the manipulations of inmates in criminal, secure hospitals, she was no stranger to the games they played. Making a mental note to tread carefully, she allowed herself to appear calm and composed as she made herself as comfortable as possible. Only when she was ready did she start the battered old tape recorder they had given her and made her introductions.

'Right, my name is Kimberley Mansfield and I'm interviewing John Smith at the Nuthall Secure Hospital. Why don't we start with a simple introduction? Can you tell me how long you've been here?'

'Straight in at the deep end, I like it!' Kimberley looked confused as John leant his elbows on the table to look at her. 'I've been a resident of this place for going on thirty-three years now.'

'Wait, that can't be right. It says here you were born October third ninety-eight nine.'

'No, that's when I arrived here.'

'It clearly says date of birth.'

'Well, that's wrong.'

Scribbling her notes, Kimberley couldn't help but stare into his eyes as he spoke.

'So, what is your date of birth?'

'April twenty-first, eighteen sixty-five.'

'Right.' Once again, Kimberley felt the fool. 'It says here you-'

'If you don't mind,' John interrupted without an apology. 'That's when I was born. What's even more interesting is the fact I died on the eighth of November eighteen-eighty eight.'

Kimberley looked up from her notes, and despite knowing he was recalling memories of a broken mind, she could tell by the look on his face that John believed what he was saying.

2

— • —

TROUBLED PAST

'I'm sure you believe what you're telling me.' Kimberley knew she was treading a fine line. Anything she said could close John up and bring her interview to an abrupt end.

'What does that paperwork say would be my cause for making it up?'

'The doctors have identified a number of diagnosis for you.'

'Care to share?' There was a nonchalant air about John as he rocked back on his chair.

'Surely your therapist has told you what they think you suffer from?'

'Schizophrenia, paranoid delusions, anxiety, autism, and a pinch of attention deficit. I expect they are somewhere on the list.'

Kimberley scanned through the documentation and found the diagnosis list she was looking for. Lifting the sheet from the file, she pushed it across the table for John to read.

'No physical contact.' The orderly's voice blared over a set of unseen speakers somewhere in the ceiling.

Flinching at the sudden voice, Kimberley looked for the source and then returned her attention to John, who simply hung his head over the paper.

'We are well aware of the rules,' John replied to the unseen speaker as he read through the printed list. 'Borderline personality disorder?'

'You disagree with it?' Kimberley pressed, seizing on John's intrigue.

Kimberley knew the dance she would have to weave in order to keep John engaged. This would be her sixteenth interview, and so far she had only gained material enough for her thesis from five of them. The others, as many did, opened up at first and then withdrew back into the protective shells they had created as a result of their disorders. Watching him read the page, Kimberley sensed there was something different. John somehow seemed more aware of himself and his surroundings than the others and yet there was something she could not put her finger on.

'I'm curious as to what it means.'

'It's a mental illness that impacts a person's ability to regulate their emotions. It's an extremely complex condition and manifests itself differently from patient to patient.'

'And you think it fits?'

'How am I supposed to make an assessment this early?' Kimberley was doing her best to be charming and John could see that. 'Maybe we can start by delving a little deeper into you.'

'I'm an open book.' John replied and sat back in the chair. 'You have everything you need to make your assessments in those censored pages.'

'Censored?'

'They're giving you pieces of the jigsaw Miss, what was your name?'

'Kimberley, but you can call me Kim if that's easier.'

'Kimberley it is then.' John offered a smile but it was impossible to read his true expression.

'You said this was censored. What would they want to keep out?'

'A very many things I would expect. I've been here such a long time I expect there are filing cabinets filled with their notes and observations, yet you get a dozen pages crammed into a brown folder in no real order.'

Kimberley had already recognised the mishmash of paperwork, but found it curious that John would be so perceptive. Balancing delicately, careful how to phrase her questions and come across, she pressed further with John.

'Would you care to tell me what you think they'd not want me to see?'

'You don't have enough time for all the details. The fact they've lied about my date of birth should have piqued your interest enough.'

'Have they though? Have they really lied or do you simply believe what you're telling me?'

'Why don't you tell me!' John leaned forward to rest his elbows on the table and stare across at her. 'You've been quick to accept the black and white writing while dismissing what I've said.'

Watching her cheeks flush, John revelled in the fact he was making her uncomfortable. Knowing the young intern would be as nervous as she had ever been, he couldn't help but admire the way she carried herself. Feeling the smallest level of remorse for being difficult, he soon changed his mind as she continued to press around his declaration about his life and death.

'It's more the fact I'm looking at a man easily in his thirties and yet you're trying to tell me you're over a hundred years old. Surely you can see that in itself would cause me to disbelieve what you're saying.'

'I thought you'd be able to see a little more when you looked. Clearly I misread you.'

'I beg your pardon!' Kimberley snapped. 'You're judging me on what, ten minutes of conversation and then complain at me for doing the same?'

Catching him by surprise, John couldn't help but smirk as Kimberley fought to regain her composure. She was quite right that John had made his early assessment of her, and so far everything she was saying and doing was confirming his assessment. Seeing her flustered was somewhat amusing and very different from what he was used to when sat in the interview room. Normally it was one of the doctors that sat on the other side of the table, expressionless and simply marching through the torrent of all too familiar questions, steering him towards the diagnosis they were intending on labelling at the start of the session.

With Kimberley, it was different. John still had no clue why the warden had allowed him to be part of her research, especially considering the fact he had been locked in the Old Wing for as long as he could remember. Still trying to decipher this curious turn of events, John realised he had indeed adopted Kimberley as nothing more than another pre-diagnosis doctor and yet, with the simplest if pushes, she had revealed emotion.

'I'm sorry,' John eventually conceded as he looked at her. 'You're right, I've judged you and I was wrong.'

Whatever wind had been in Kimberley's sails evaporated, leaving her open-mouthed on the other side of the table. Giving her a moment to compose herself, John reached over and took a second sheet from Kimberley's side of the table.

'No, I shouldn't have snapped. That wasn't very professional of me.'

'You probably shouldn't, but it at least tells me you're human.' John offered his reply without lifting his attention from the printed sheet. 'Shall we continue?'

'Yes.' Once again composed, Kimberley lifted her gaze and waited for him to speak.

'So, where do you want this to go?'

'I'd like to find out more about you. Why you're here, what you know about what's happened to you and things like that.'

'I've already told you how long I've been here, but you chose not to believe that part.' Quick to compliment the remark with a wry smile, John didn't give her a chance to reply. 'Let's pretend that you believed me. What would you ask me next?'

'I'd start by asking if you knew what year it was.'

'Sometime around twenty-twenty, I would assume.'

'I'd ask you what it was like where you grew up.' Feeling she was being guided down the path John wanted to take, Kimberley knew better than to resist.

'London was a cold place back then. I remember winters being bitter. Sometime around my tenth birthday, I remember Mrs Creswell, our neighbour, dying. In my head she froze to death, but I think truth be told, she just had her time.'

'And where abouts in London did you live?'

'All over. My dad went where the factory work took him. But I spent most of my time in Whitechapel.'

Knowing there would be clues to the truth, Kimberley scribbled down notes as John continued to answer her questions. Occasionally, she would latch onto a phrase or word and circle it to come back to later. Having danced like this before, Kimberley's tutor had taught her to piece together the jigsaw pieces as a broken mind slowly opened up. Having sat through many lectures, she knew the pieces were scattered and while fanciful, there would be anchors to the truth in what John was telling her.

'Were you in the factories too, like your dad?'

'No.' John took a moment to draw the memories back. 'He wanted more for me than the life of a factory worker. I went on to join the Metropolitan Police, something my dad wasn't a big fan of, but it was better than the factories.'

'The police? What made you choose that?'

'A sense of purpose, I suppose.' John toyed with the handcuffs around his wrists. 'Seems ironic, all things considered.'

'I won't say I believe what you're saying, but I believe you do.' Kimberley looked up from her notes. 'If you're alright talking about it, I'd like to ask some more questions and see if I can't get through what you believe is true and find what is actually the truth?'

'Whatever you like, Kimberley, I'm happy for you to waste some time trying to decipher something that isn't there.'

'Did you have any siblings?'

'No, I was an only child. My dad got injured in the factory after I was born, almost killed him, but it meant he couldn't have any more children.'

'And your mother?'

'She was lost.' John struggled to hide the sudden wave of pain that boiled from his stomach. 'She did everything she could to support my old man, but she had her demons. The year I joined the police, they found her in the Thames, drowned in a drunken stupor.'

John fought to hide back the sea of emotion that consumed him. Grateful for the respectful silence, John watched as Kimberley scribbled a handful of notes on her paper. When she had finished writing, he had composed himself enough to carry on.

'How did that affect you, your mother's death?'

'I threw myself into work. Dad took it bad. He did the same, and we drifted apart. I found a new family in the police and wanted to make her proud.'

'I'm sure she was.'

'I'm sure she was a drunk who wouldn't care less.' John's sudden cold reply caught Kimberley by surprise. 'I appreciate the sympathy, I really do, but I've lived long enough to realise that she was gone because of the life choices she made. It may sound cold and callous, but it's the bitter truth of it all. Yes, at the time, I thought I was making her proud, but having had time to think about it, that was the whimsical dreams of an immature young man.'

'I think we should move past that then.' Kimberley offered, once again circling a word in the centre of the page. 'What about your job? What did you do in the police?'

'Maybe I should show you.'

'I beg your pardon.'

'I'm not blind. I can see your expression and maybe the only way I can convince you is to show you.'

'And how would you do that?'

Kimberley felt a wave of unease as John shuffled to sit on the edge of his seat and placed both his hands down on the table. Rolling up his sleeves, Kimberley noticed a jet-black bird in mid flight on his right forearm.

'What type of bird is that?'

'It's a raven, but that will all make sense when I show you.' John wiggled his fingers, making it appear that the inked raven was moving on his flesh. 'Take my hands and I will show you.'

'We can't do that.'

'Did you ask yourself why they told you that?'

'Because you could be dangerous.'

'I have no desire to hurt you. All I want you to do is believe me, and the only way to do that is to show you.'

'I don't understand how you can do that.'

Despite her screaming senses, Kimberley felt herself drawn to John's open hands. She had seen nothing in the paperwork, but more importantly nothing for John himself, that showed he would hurt her. Against her better judgement, she placed the pen down on the pad and moved one hand across the table.

'If you can believe I'm over a hundred years old, you can believe I have the means to show you.'

Almost reaching his hands, Kimberley stopped herself and met John's gaze. Hand still hovering over the table, she looked deep into his eyes and longed to see an answer. Knowing she was overstepping, Kimberley changed her mind and knew she had to bring the conversation back. Moving her hand away, Kimberley screamed in terror as John lurched forward and grabbed her wrist and hand in a vice-like grip.

'Let me show you.'

Unable to make a sound, the terrified shriek somehow lost in her throat, Kimberly felt the world around her close in as a wave of darkness washed over her. Like falling into an uncomfortable sleep, the world went dark and all she could hear was the sound of her ragged breaths as panic set in.

3

— • —

MEMORIES OF THE PAST

WHITECHAPEL, LONDON - NOVEMBER 1th 1888

Kimberley sensed the darkness around her, and slowly her senses returned. Watching her on the ground, John admired his surroundings as Kimberley slowly came to.

John was standing in an open square in the heart of Victorian London. Painted in the pale glow of a full moon, the city was dark and dreary. Still dressed in his hospital fatigues, he looked out-of-place considering his surroundings, but none of the passing people paid him any attention. Looking up to the jagged skyline of pitched rooftops, he heard Kimberley groan and returned his attention to her.

'Take a moment. You'll be a little disorientated at first.'

'Where am I? What's happening?' Ripping open her eyes, there was a look of pure panic on her young face.

'Relax. I told you I would show you.'

'This isn't possible. Where are we?'

'You're in my memories.'

'Utter crap!' Kimberley snapped as she got to her feet.

Unsteady and staggering a little, John moved to offer her a hand, but she quickly retracted away from him. Eyes wide and senses overcome by her newfound surroundings, John gave her a moment to drink in gothic Victorian London. Feeling very much at home, John turned to look towards the silhouette of Big Ben in the distance. He had spent many hours reliving his memories of London, much preferring it to what he had last experienced of the city before he had been locked inside the Nuthall Hospital.

Closing his eyes for a moment, he allowed his senses to fill with the chatter of voices and the echo of hooves on the cobbled roads. He felt home, as if the city was somehow welcoming him with its warm embrace, wrapping around him like a comfort blanket.

'I need to go back.' Kimberley gasped as she clutched at her throat. 'I can't breathe. Please.'

'There's nothing wrong with you.' John sighed as he kept his eyes closed and turned his head to the bright moon. 'You're mind is simply fighting what I knows can't be true. Give it a moment.'

'I don't want to give it a moment. I want to go back.'

Feeling her fingers grasp at his back, John turned around to look at her. Still clutching at her throat, Kimberley turned away and stalked towards a crowd of young women gathered outside the door to a quaint pub.

'They can't see you.' John warned as Kimberley tried to touch the trio of women but saw her hand pass through them like ghosts.

'Help me.' She screamed as she recoiled away from the spectral figures. 'Take me back. Take me back.'

Spinning on the spot, John closed her down in two long strides and took hold of her shoulders. Stopping her still, he removed her hand from her throat and held her gaze.

'Calm down. You need to take a moment to acclimatise to what's just happened.'

'I can't.

John waited. Knowing what it felt like, he had to let her body come to terms with the impossibility of its situation before she would be able to calm down. After what felt like an age, the expression of panic faded from her face and Kimberley once again regained a modicum of her composure. Enough at least to pull herself free from John's grasp and stare at him from a safer distance.

'This is London, the day of my death.'

'We've gone back in time?'

'Not at all, my dear.' John chuckled. 'This is simply my memory.'

'Oh, simply? Simply your memory. That makes it all okay, then.' Kimberley was fighting to keep herself calm. 'How have you done this?'

'We will get to that in a moment.'

'We'll get to it now!'

'No.' John replied, his voice flat and emotionless. 'This isn't the time. Now is the time to watch him.'

Beyond all realm of possibility, Kimberley turned and saw John Smith, dressed as a police constable, saunter into the open square. Looking somewhat cleaner and better presented, John had a handsome air about him as he walked towards a well-dressed gentleman standing in the shadows on the other side of the street. Passing by the three women outside the pub, they saw the approaching policeman and quickly scurried away into the night.

'That's you!' Kimberley exclaimed as she watched the alternate version of John move in front of her. 'You've not aged a day.'

'Why would I?' John scoffed as he moved to follow his other self. 'This is the day I died. You don't tend to get much older after that point.'

The fact John was so flippant caught Kimberley by surprise and she could see he was getting some level of amusement out of everything that was happening. Taking his lead, they followed to the meeting. As the past version of John approached the well-dressed gentleman, his face was illuminated for a second as he lit a cigarette between his lips.

'Inspector.' John offered as he approached.

'Mr Smith, how very good it is to see you out and about. Anything to report?'

'Nothing, sir. The streets have been a lot quieter, not to say I think we've banished the Ripper by any stretch of the imagination.'

'The Ripper, as in Jack The Ripper?' Kimberley hissed.

'Hush, just listen.' Motioning towards the two men, John returned his attention to the hushed conversation.

'The newspapers have gone quiet on the story. Fed, I expect, from the powers that be to return London to a state of calm.'

'But he's still on the loose, isn't he?' The younger John pressed the senior officer. 'Why hasn't he killed again?'

'That, my dear boy, I can't fathom. Such a violent spree and then nothing for almost a year.' Removing a pocket watch, the inspector checked the time and stepped down from the doorway. 'Do your rounds and be vigilant.'

'I will do Inspector.'

'Find me at the end of your shift. I have something I wish to discuss with you.' Before the younger John could press further, the older Inspector turned and stalked away along the now quiet street.

'I always wanted to know what he was going to talk to me about. I never made it to the meeting.'

'Why not?'

'Because, if you care to keep up, this is where I died.'

Despite the playfulness of his tone, Kimberley was still struggling to comprehend what was happening. As John set off in the wake of his past self, Kimberley pinched the back of her hand as if hoping she would wake from this crazy dream. Finding no change to her surroundings, she quickly made her choice and fell into step by John's side.

Struggling to keep pace, they moved with haste along the labyrinth of streets until they emerged into another vast open square, this time dominated by an impressive water fountain. While the shadows they passed were alive with movement and faces, wherever the uniformed constable moved, the people disappeared from view. It was clear that his presence was not welcome and more than once Kimberley thought she saw a figure stalking them from the shadows as they passed by the open alleys around the edge of the square.

'Follow me, we'll have an excellent position from over there.' John pointed to the churning water feature.

'Shouldn't we stay with him, I mean you?'

'It all happens here, and I would hate for you to miss it.'

The chimes of Big Ben carried in the air, encouraging John to move with haste towards the fountain.

'What happens?'

'Everything I told you will come to pass in this moment.'

On cue, a sickening scream pierced the air, and all attention turned towards a narrow alley on the far side of the square. The younger apparition of John froze on the spot and snatched his attention around in the sound's direction. Ripping the truncheon from his belt, he moved towards the dark alley with the weapon held in front of him.

'Police, show yourself.' John's voice quivered as he made his announcement. 'Step out from there.'

Standing a little away from the mouth of the alley, John waited for any indication the source of the noise had heard him. Getting no response, he inched closer and peered into the shadows. Nothing moved in the darkness. Somehow the shadows seemed darker and as he moved closer, the faint sounds of ragged breaths carried in the air towards him.

'Show yourself I say. Stop messing around.'

The shadows somehow grew from the alley, stretching like fingers from the darkness until they reached John's boots. Unnerved by the strangeness, he unconsciously took a step back and turned his attention back to the opening. As if growing from the shadow itself, a figure moved and took shape in front of him.

'Come out, slowly.' John warned as the enormous figure took shape in the shadows.

What emerged from the alley was not human. Although it had the shape of a man, the figure towered over John as it sauntered into the open square. Somehow the figure looked to be made of shadow and even the dancing light from the nearby streetlight could not pierce the darkness that surrounded its body. Putting space between him and the creature, John's eyes were wide as the figure changed and its features slowly came into view.

With broad shoulders and narrow waist, the figure looked powerful and imposing. A top hat was perched on its head and while the shadows clung to it, the features it allowed to be seen showed oversized muscles straining to break free of the ill-fitting

Victorian top hat and tails. Despite the ludicrous nature of a seven-foot tall giant emerging from the shadows in an ill-fitting suit, John could feel nothing but terror as he tripped over his own feet and crashed to the ground.

'What is that?' Kimberley gasped as the darkness melted away from the creature and its face came into view.

All charred skin and scars, a pair of lifeless eyes looked out from its sunken sockets.

'That is the Ripper.' John replied, his voice barely above a whisper.

'It can't be.' Kimberley protested as the Ripper moved to stand over the younger John. 'The Ripper was a man, the Queen's surgeon, or a butcher, wasn't he?'

'It was very much a butcher, but not in the sense they have led you to believe. That *is* the Ripper.'

Before she could ask any more questions, John on the ground screamed and scurried away as the enormous creature slammed a foot down onto the back of his leg. Hearing the bone break, Kimberley yelped in sympathy as the injured John grasped at his snapped lower leg. Fighting to pull his whistle from his breast pocket, John fought to squeeze it between his lips and prepared to blow.

Wrapping its hands around John's neck, Kimberley watched as it hoisted the younger man into the air to hang like a limp doll, his broken leg swaying painfully side to side.

'Do something.' Kimberley demanded as she tugged at John's arm.

'This isn't something I can change. This is just a memory.' John's attention was fixed on the Ripper. 'Just watch, as I have a thousand times.'

Fighting against the vice-like grip of the Ripper, the younger John managed to pull himself free and dropped to the ground. Unable to support his own weight, John crumpled to the floor, and the Ripper was once again upon him in a heartbeat.

'Who are you?' John stammered as he desperately dragged himself across the cobbled street.

'I am the darkness,' the Ripper replied, its booming voice echoing around the square. 'And you are nothing.'

Taking hold of John's leg, the Ripper hoisted him into the air as if he was weightless. Unable to fight back, John was powerless as the Ripper clenched its fist and slammed a heavy blow into John's stomach. Releasing his grasp at the same time, the younger John was launched through the air to come crashing into the ornate stone fountain at Kimberley's feet.

'Help him!'

'There is no helping.' John replied as the Ripper stalked over to him.

Something changed in John's demeanour as the memory played out before them. Reaching John, the Ripper dropped to its haunches and moved closer to the panting constable. Speaking so only John could hear, the Ripper offered its final words.

'Your death will serve no purpose. I have had my fill and this will be a pointless death.'

In one swift move, the Ripper delivered the final blow. Unable to watch, Kimberley turned away, but the sickening sound told her all she needed. The sound of bone crunching and the harsh escape of breath indicated that the Ripper had indeed killed John. Hearing the Ripper's footsteps moving back across the square, Kimberley turned her attention back to John's lifeless corpse at her feet.

Young, lifeless, and broken. John's eyes were wide and unmoving as the dead officer's body was bathed in the sickening pale moonlight.

'I want to go.' Kimberley stammered.

'Not yet.' John soothed as he looked down at his own dead body. 'There's something more you need to see.'

4

DEATH COMES FOR US ALL

As the demonic Ripper returned to the safety of the alley, Kimberley dropped down from her seat and moved to look at John's body.

'Why aren't you going to do something?'

Joining her, John took hold of her arm and dragged her away from the lifeless corpse. Struggling against his grip, Kimberley fought to break free, but stopped when a sudden rumble of thunder carried in the air. Despite the cloudless sky, there was no denying what she had heard as she scanned around for the source of the sound. Seeing nothing, Kimberley sensed they were not alone and expected the Ripper to once again emerge from the alley in search of them.

'There's nothing to do except to watch.'

On the other side of the square, something moved and as Kimberley directed her attention towards the movement, the impossible happened. From nowhere, a figure appeared out of thin air, a figure familiar to Kimberley, and yet it was something she had never seen before. The new arrival appeared on the move and walked casually across the cobbled square towards John's lifeless body.

As Kimberley drank in the stranger's appearance, her brain tried to make sense of what she was seeing. Dressed in a long, flowing black robe, there was no denying what it was. Carrying a scythe in one hand, tapping the base on the ground with every other step, this was Death. Arriving at John's body, the spectre of the Grim Reaper hovered for a moment before tapping the corpse with the base of the scythe. As the wooden handle nudged the body, Kimberley gasped at what happened.

While John's body remained unmoving on the ground, somehow his spirit emerged from the shell and rose to its feet.

'What's happened to me?' John's spirit gasped as it looked up at the visage of Death.

'Well dear boy, there's no easy way to put this. You're dead.'

Death's voice was oddly calm and matter of fact. From beneath the darkness of the hood, Kimberley could make out nothing of his facial features, and watched as John's spirit eyed Death with an air of suspicion.

'Just who the hell are you?'

'Oh come now, look at your feet and you'll see what I'm telling you.'

Dropping his gaze to his own body, John recoiled away in horror. Overcome with terror, John comically looked from his body, to Death and back again. Watching his reactions, John could not help but feel a wave of sympathy and embarrassment at his completely dumbfounded reaction. At last, John's spirit settled its attention on Death and waited for an answer.

'How...why...who?'

'Don't worry, this is an entirely natural reaction. Here, let me make it a little easier to talk.'

Pulling the hood from his head, Kimberley shrieked as she saw the floating skull in the pale moonlight. Illuminating the pale mottled bone, Kimberley watched as skin grew from the dark recesses of the skull. Crawling to cover the entire skull, all eyes watched as Death's face took shape into something more recognisable and human. A handsome man in his late fifties, Death sported a neatly trimmed goatee and rich green eyes that scanned around the empty London street.

'How?'

'Please, can we have questions longer than a single word?'

'I'm sorry, it's just that, well surely you can understand why I'm shocked?'

'You're not the first, and won't be the last.' Death smiled. 'But I'm here for a different reason than you might expect.'

'What is that?'

'I'll begin by telling you it wasn't your time.' Death rolled John's body onto its back and bent down to admire his wide-eyed face.

Seeing the moon reflected in his lifeless eyes, Death lowered his gloved hand to John's face and closed the dead man's eyelids out of respect. Muttering something under his breath, Death loitered for a moment before returning his attention to John's spirit.

'If it wasn't my time, can't I go back?'

'It's not that simple, my dear boy, I'm afraid not.' Death moved away from the body and loitered at the edge of the fountain. 'The moment of transition from life has been done. There is no way to send you back and yet your soul has no judgement to be made.'

'Judgement?'

'A long story dear boy, one for another time.'

'Then why are you here? If you're not going to answer my questions, is it just the fact you're here to take me to wherever it is I am supposed to go?'

'You have no place.' Death sighed as his fingers dragged through the water despite there being no reflection of him on the glassy surface. 'That's what has drawn me to this moment, to your death.'

'Speak sense!' John's spirit snapped. 'Nothing you're saying is making any sense.'

'Your lifeline was longer than this moment. I have seen you in passing and knew our paths were not destined to cross for many years to come and yet here we stand.' Death toyed with his beard for a moment before continuing. 'Whatever stole the life from you left a darker mark than I have seen in many years.'

'You mean the Ripper? He did this!'

'Is that what you call it?'

'It, no, him! The Ripper has been preying on the women in this city for the past few years.'

'That creature is not a him. That thing is a demon, born from the fires of Sub Terra and roaming the earth, feeding off the living.'

'Sub what?'

'We don't have time for an explanation of the world I inhabit, just enough to make you an offer.'

'What sort of offer?'

'You present me with an opportunity, one I have not come across in my time as the Reaper.' Death moved closer and stood almost nose-to-nose with John's spirit. 'Being taken before your time, I have the chance to give you an opportunity to stop that thing before it kills again.'

'Then I'll do it,' John interrupted. 'I've seen what it has done. It needs to be stopped.'

'Don't be so quick to commit yourself to this. What I offer you is not a simply act of vengeance, I offer you the opportunity to be my hand.'

'Your hand?'

'I find it concerning that creatures like this can exist in the living world and move without leaving a trace, I can see. It would appear I am in need of someone with a connection to that world, and so I find myself talking to you.'

'Can I stop him from killing again? That's all that matters.'

'I will give you the power to face it, yes. Whether you succeed will be down to you. All I can do is give you the tools. You must put them to use.'

'Then I'll do it.'

'You wear that uniform well.' Death grinned as he replaced the hood over his head, once again disguising his face in the deep shadows of the fabric. 'Perhaps I should fashion you a new one.'

Without warning, Death took John's spirit by the collar and lifted him into the air. Rising like a spectre, Kimberley craned her neck to watch as the pair rose higher into the air above the empty square. Unable to hear what was being said, Kimberley and John could only watch as Death performed the ritual.

'Your soul is clean, untainted and too early for the afterlife.' Death hissed, his voice no longer calm and soothing. 'Do you swear to be the hand of Death, sworn protector of the living against the forces of darkness that would seek to disrupt the balance?'

'Yes.' John answered, his arms hanging loosely by his side.

Ignoring the fact he was now floating high above the ground and faced with the empty hood of the Grim Reaper, John closed his eyes and made his promise.

'Do you forfeit your transference in service as Death's Hand?'

'Yes.'

'You are to be reborn, my agent, my hand.' Moving higher into the air, the street looked tiny below as John dared to open his eyes. 'You are reborn, the Raven.'

Releasing John from his grip, Death watched as the startled young man dropped like a stone towards the ground. Dragged down by gravity and unable to stop the fall, John screamed in terror. Hearing his cries, Kimberley turned away, not wanting to see him crash to the ground. Instead of hearing a heavy *thud*, Kimberley heard nothing. After what felt like an age, she turned her attention back to the square and gasped at what she saw.

Where Kimberley had expected to see John's spirit in a crumpled mess on the ground, she saw something entirely different. No longer dressed in his uniform, John had taken on the appearance of the Raven. Dressed in a long black coat adorned with brass buttons, over a waistcoat and mishmash of belts and buttons, John stood proud and tall with a dark hood over his head. Turning to face the pair at the fountain, Kimberley was surprised to see his face concealed beneath an ornate plague doctor's mask.

'What have you done to me?' John hollered, his voice muffled by the leather and brass mask covering his face.

'I've given you the means with which to fight this evil.' Death replied as he lowered down to the ground. 'Now, do me proud.'

With nothing else to add, Death moved to the fountain and joined Kimberley and John as they watched the Raven take in his new appearance. Curious and unnerved by the visage of Death by her side, Kimberley chanced a glance out the corner of her eye and jumped as she realised the empty hood was facing directly at her.

'You'll enjoy this part, Kimberley.' Death hissed from under the hood. 'John remembers it like it's yesterday, don't you?'

'That I do.'

'I thought this was a memory,' Kimberley protested as she snatched her attention around to John. 'How is he speaking to us?'

'Some things just don't have an explanation.' John replied with a wink.

Kimberley was about to protest when she heard the familiar sound of the Ripper's footsteps behind her. Turning around to face back into the square, once again the shadows seeped out of the alley as the Ripper stepped into view. As before, the oversized creature walked tall and with an air of unshaking confidence. Bathed in the moonlight, the Ripper's physique rippled in the light and once again the lifeless eyes glared from their sunken sockets in the Raven's direction.

'What is this thing you offer me, Azrael?'

'The means to send you back to where you belong.' Death replied as he rested his scythe by his side and leaned back against the stone fountain casually. 'You displace the balance and I must return in kind.'

'A fledgling creature of your creation?' The Ripper chortled as it stalked across the cobbled square. 'A short amusement he will give me, I'm sure.'

'Your reign of terror and death is over.' John, the Raven, declared from beneath the plague mask.

'Is this some fancy dress parade?' The Ripper mocked as it came to a halt in front of him. 'Here I stand before you, proud and in my true form. And yet you stand before me like a whore at a party.'

'That may be the case, but I'm putting an end to your murderous campaign of terror.'

Stretching out both hands to his sides, a pair of escrima sticks appeared in each of the Raven's hands. Each of the weapons were gloss black with brilliant red lettering in an unfamiliar language. Testing the weight of the wooden weapons, he rotated them around and took up a defensive stance, both weapons pointed towards the Ripper.

'Oh, now this will be fun.' The Ripper smirked, its charred skin twitching in the moonlight. 'You should probably change your mind.'

'Not going to happen.'

'So be it.'

Twisting away, the Ripper was the first to attack as it lowered its weight and launched through the air towards the newly born Raven. Prepared for whatever was to come, John, in his form as Death's Hand, was ready to do what he must. As Kimberley, John and Death looked on, a fight between undead creatures had begun.

5

A RAVEN'S BIRTH

The Ripper's attack was furious and relentless. Having launched through the air, he delivered a powerful blow that pushed the Raven back across the square. Using the escrima sticks in his defence, the Raven halted his movements and raised his gaze to the Ripper. Having timed his attack, the Ripper lurched forward, dragging a powerful fist behind him. Timed to perfection, the enormous clenched fist slammed into the Raven's chest.

Too slow to react, the power of the attack launched him through the air, sending him flying into the stone base of the fountain. Crashing into the structure, the stone splintered and water cascaded through the jagged gap created by the Raven's landing. Soaked and shaken by the ferocity of the attack, he rose to his knees and peered across at his opponent.

'Why doesn't he fight?' Kimberley hissed.

'I am fighting.' John replied as he watched his past self rise to his feet.

Brushing off the water from his coat, he intercepted the next attack as the Ripper lurched forward. Deflecting the heavy fist, his return blow sent him rotating away. Slamming the wooden weapon into the side of the Ripper's head, the Raven felt a rush of pride as the top hat tumbled to the floor.

Taking a moment, the Raven took in the Ripper's appearance. No longer shrouded in the shadow of the tall hat, the Ripper's face was now exposed for all to see. A face of mottled, charred flesh. What had appeared to be hair was, in fact, a pair of crooked horns that had been grown over the top and down the back of his head. Turned up at the ends, the horns were ridged, giving it the appearance of slick-back hair.

'You fight well.' The Ripper snarled. 'Perhaps I should show you the true depth of my power.'

Clenching both fists, they all watched as the Ripper's body became lined with veins of pale pink light. Covering every inch of its body, the Ripper appeared to grow as the light moved up its body and into its eyes. Taking full advantage of the distraction, it once again attacked and barreled down a barrage of blows towards the Raven.

The fight raged across the entire square as neither creature of the afterlife was able to find advantage over the other. Despite the ferocious battle between them, the street remained empty of bystanders, leaving only Kimberley, John, and Death watching from the sidelines. Taking hold of the Raven, the Ripper hammered a trio of blows down onto his head, dislodging the plague mask. Tearing the leather mask from his head, the Ripper tossed it across the square and glared down at John's exposed face.

'Just a man.'

'Just a monster.' John snarled and drove the escrima stick up, connecting with the Ripper's chin.

Knocking his head back, forced back by the force of the blow, the Ripper released its grip on him and staggered away. Releasing a deep roar of frustration, the Ripper was quick to regain its composure.

'Call me what you will, this is my playground and no menial servant of him will stop me.' The Ripper pointed towards Death. 'You have sealed your own fate to an eternity of nothingness by challenging me.'

'He's done nothing of the sort.' Death replied from the sidelines. 'Now, if you wouldn't mind I'd appreciate you not embarrassing me by losing.'

Death's joviality caught Kimberley by surprise, but his words were enough to spurn the Raven to attack. Taking full advantage of the distraction, he moved with astonishing speed as he launched through the air and took the Ripper completely unaware. Driving the escrima sticks up and around, both weapons found their mark and forced the Ripper to go on the defence.

Shielding its face from the flurry of attack as, more than once, the sticks found their mark. So close to it, John could almost taste the fetid stench of death and decay that hung around the Ripper. Passing through the smell, he pressed on harder until the Ripper caught his right arm as he moved to deliver another attack.

'Fairer without these.' The Ripper snatched the stick from his grasp and tossed it across the square.

Moving to pull himself free, the second stick was yanked from his grasp, rendering him unarmed. Still holding his wrist, the Ripper slammed his head into John's maskless face, sending stars dancing in his vision. Fighting to break free, their combat became more brutal and desperate. Crashing his elbow into the Ripper's jaw, John heard a satisfying *crack* and, propelled by the momentum, John could pull himself free.

Spinning away, his long coat spreading out as he moved, John put enough distance between them and took a moment to settle his vision. As the world came into focus and blinking lights faded, he saw that his attack had dislodged the Ripper's lower jaw, which now hung at a jaunty and unnatural position. Taking hold of it, John could hear the sickening scraping of bone on bone as the Ripper returned his jaw back into position.

Not wasting time, John launched his next foray of attacks and this time allowed his newfound powers to take hold. Reaching the Ripper, John felt a sensation in his legs and launched the pair of them up into the air. Whatever strength had been contained in his muscles carried them high above the rooftops of the surrounding buildings. With the expanse of Victorian London in view, the majestic beauty of the moonlit capital almost distracted John.

Sensing another impending attack, John rotated over in the air and drove them back towards the ground. Forcing the Ripper beneath him, their momentum grew as the ground approached. Colliding with the floor, cobbles and roadway splintered by the sheer force of their landing and John was able to roll away unscathed.

'Good skills.' Death yelled his approval as the Ripper pulled away the debris that covered his torso.

Enraged by the sudden turn of events, he launched from the shallow crater and the fight between them resumed. Blow after blow, they fought with renewed ferocity until, at last, the Ripper gained an advantage. Wrapping its arms around John's waist, he was powerless to resist as the Ripper raised him over his head and dropped backwards, slamming his head onto the cobbles.

Pinned to the ground, the Ripper stamped down onto the side of John's head and pressed his weight down. Unable to move, John scratched and pulled to rip the dead weight free. The only release came as the Ripper raised his foot and stamped down over and over again until the world began to close in around him.

As his vision faded, each blow brought a memory flashing through his mind. The first he saw was his mother's body laid on the mortuary slab, her skin pale and soaked from the Thames.

Another blow brought another memory. This time it was his graduation into the police, a moment of immense pride overshadowed by the broken appearance of his father at the back of the room, unable to meet his gaze.

'I have no son.' His father's voice echoed in his head, bouncing around like he was right beside him.

'Time to die again!' The Ripper screamed and stamped down one last time.

The memory that consumed John was a series of flashing moments from the crime scenes of the Ripper. Each gruesome murder scene was etched in his mind, vivid and alive, as if he were there again. The women's youth and pain were painted around the room in scenes that were fit for nightmares. Knowing he had failed them, failed to protect the scores of victims that the Ripper would undoubtedly create, in light of his failure.

'I chose you for a reason.' Death's voice hissed, barely above a whisper in his senses. 'This thing will walk free if you don't succeed. I gave the power to protect those people, to protect those who cannot do it themselves. Now get it and end this.'

Feeling a jolt of electricity through his body, every nerve tingling from his head to his toe, John opened his eyes and pushed back. Whatever strength bubbled inside him was enough to break free of the Ripper's pressure. Moving the foot enough, John pushed away and rolled clear. Sweeping the Ripper's legs from beneath him, John snatched up one of the discarded escrima sticks and drove it through the air, burying it into the Ripper's chest.

Letting out a blood-curdling scream, the Ripper staggered away, clutching at the wood protruding at an awkward angle from its barrelled chest. Finding no purchase, the Ripper's chest glowed around the entry wound and John watched as its actions became more frenzied. Clawed fingers struggling, John could only watch until he heard Death's voice in his ear.

Appearing at his side, the shrouded visage of the hooded Grim Reaper leaned closer, so only John could hear his hushed words.

'Finish what you have started. Send it back to the shadows, free the living from this monster.'

'Why don't you do it?' John snapped, his attention fixed on the flailing Ripper.

'That is not my purpose. I transition undecided souls for judgement but you, you are my sentinel against the growing darkness.' Placing his gloved hand on John's shoulder, he offered him the discarded plague doctor mask. 'Take it, become the sentinel the world needs. Be my hand and do what I cannot.'

Dropping his gaze to the leather mask, John hesitated. Ignoring the Ripper, he saw his reflection in the blue tinted lenses covering the eye-pieces of the mask.

'Will I ever feel again?' John quizzed, his voice hoarse and dry.

'You are something else now, a spirit between this life and the next. You'll find a way to accept that.'

'Like you have?'

'Take it, become the Raven.' Stepping away, he left John admiring the intricately crafted plague mask.

Taking in a deep breath, John placed the mask over his face and allowed his vision to adjust to the blue hue of the lenses. As the smell of the leather invaded his senses, he made his choice and charged towards the Ripper. Still overcome with frenzy, it was powerless to do anything as the flesh of its chest now smouldered around the protruding weapon.

Reaching the demon, John drove down his weight onto the wooden stick, sending the Ripper crashing to the ground beneath him. Putting all his weight on the stick, it sank deeper into its chest. Pressing the hooked nose of the plague mask into the face of the snarling demon, John chose his last words carefully.

'Your reign of terror in my city is over.' John spat, his words filled with venom and hate. 'Go back to the darkness from where you came.'

Hammering a fist down, the air was filled with a deafening clap of thunder. The Ripper's body exploded in a cloud of black smoke, the force of which sent John flying backwards through the air. Rather than crashing to the ground this time, John landed with poise a handful of feet away from where the Ripper had been. As the smoke dissipated, John could only see the discarded weapon lying on the cobbled street with no sign of the twisted Ripper, only the tendrils of shadow retreating back along the square.

'Is it dead?' John asked as he turned towards the fountain where Death was sat.

'It was never alive.'

'Is it gone then?'

'That creature no longer stalks the shadows.'

'Then I'm done?'

'You already know the answer to that, my Raven.' Death clambered down from his perch atop the fountain. 'There will always be the demons in the shadows, and they will always need you to protect them.'

Before John could offer any retort, Death disappeared, leaving only John and the two unseen observers in the empty square.

'What happens next?' Kimberley asked as she looked at the John she knew from the hospital.

'This is where this memory ends. We should get back.'

Almost tenderly, John touched her cheek and in a heartbeat she felt herself ripped from where she was sat.

6

THE FEAR OF KNOWING

NUTHALL SECURE HOSPITAL, LONDON

Kimberley launched back away from the table, eyes wide and brow drenched with sweat. Wiping the back of her hand across her forehead, she pressed back away from the table until she reached the secured door.

'Calm down.' John pressed as he dropped his hands back to the table. 'You're going to draw attention.'

'Get me out of here!' Kimberley shrieked as she hammered her fists on the inside of the door.

'Or else shout like that and they'll come running.'

'Help!'

'Really, you're shouting for help?' John sighed as he slumped back in the chair and waited for the door to burst open.

Moving aside as the door was unlocked from the outside, Kimberley burst past the orderly and disappeared along the corridor. Leaning his head back, John looked up at the ceiling and let out a long, exacerbated sigh.

'Messed around with another one?' The orderly tutted as he pulled the door shut. 'The warden won't be so quick to let you have visitors again. Back to the shadows for you, John.'

Watching the door close, John kept his attention on the flickering bulb behind the plexi-glass in the ceiling. Listening to the locking mechanism secure the door, he waited a few moments before bringing his gaze back down into the room.

'Are you going to join me, or hide in the shadows?' John asked the empty room. 'I know you still watch me. How else would you have spoken to her in my memories?'

His questions went unanswered, as they always did, when he attempted to speak to Death. It had been a good number of years since Death had spoken back and while John could feel his presence, there was some invisible block between him and the one that made him in his image. Testing the strength of the chains and cuffs, John eyed the scattered papers that littered the table. When Kimberley had made her hasty exit from the interview room, a handful of sheets had tumbled to the ground. Peering around the side of the table, John's attention fell to a folded newspaper clipping.

Eyeing it with suspicion, the paper was out of his reach. Shuffling to the edge of his seat, he fought to drag the clipping back with his shoes. Straining against the restraints, John finally pinned the paper beneath the sole of his shoe and moved it towards him. When it was finally in reach, he scooped it up and unfolded it on the metal table in front of him.

'This can't be.' John gasped as he read the headline.

IS JACK BACK? NEW RIPPER STALKS LONDON

Reading through the article, what colour was left in John's face drained away. Every word filled him with a sense of fear and dread. Re-reading it, John learned of the latest series of grisly murders that had been reported by the police. Reminiscent of the urban legend of Jack The Ripper, the level of detail in the article left little to the imagination. All at once, the memories of the murders he had witnessed came flooding back. Pushing back from the table, John's eyes were wide with panic as the door to the interview room burst open.

'Warden's decided some time in solitary might serve you well.' The orderly declared as he stalked into the room, followed by two other staff members.

Grabbing the cutting from the table, John stuffed it into his pocket and quickly raised his hands.

'I'm not going to put up a fight.'

'Oh, please do.' The orderly smirked as he pulled an extendable baton from the back of his trousers.

Knowing what was coming, John longed to fight back, but knew the risks. His whispered oath with death meant he was to protect the living, not bring them to Death's door before their time. Knowing what he had once been capable of, John simply sat back in the seat and waited for the barrage of abuse that he knew was coming. The first strike came from the side and sent him crashing to the floor. Still shackled to the table, John curled himself into a ball and accepted the beating.

***

Kimberley burst into her apartment and stormed across the open plan living room to rest against the panoramic window. Now bathed in darkness, the shimmering city lights were hazy against the low hanging fog that had settled for the evening. Having hastily left the Nuthall Hospital, she had made it through the underground and found herself swept along with the sea of people in rush hour. Not knowing what to do, her head racing in a million directions, she had found a quiet corner and waited for the swarms of people to lessen before making her way home.

Even thinking about the impossibility of what she had seen sent cold shivers through her body. With her head buried in her hand, the screaming and rumbling of the approaching train had brought her back from replaying the disturbing memory of events. Boarding, she had made her way home and felt a wave of relief to at last be in the safety of her apartment.

Pulling a chair close to the window, Kimberley dropped into the seat and stared out of the window. Sat in the darkness, she looked at the flowing traffic far below in the streets and tried to make sense of everything. Snatching a notepad from the coffee table behind her, Kimberley set about making notes of what she remembered. Key elements, images, words spoken and, above all, the look of what she had seen.

As the hours passed by, she filled more and more pages with rough sketches and lines of text recounting what she had seen.

When sleep finally swallowed her, dragging her into an uneasy rest, the pad dropped into her lap with the last image she had sketched in smudged ink of The Raven.

'You were in such a rush to leave.' John's voice whispered from the shadows of her apartment. 'I'd have hoped to speak to you more.'

Hearing the voice, Kimberley's eyes ripped open, and she launched from the chair, dropping the pad as she moved. Scanning the dark apartment, her heart pounded in her eyes as she tried to shake off the dizziness from her startled awakening.

'Who's there?'

'Well, I would think that was obvious!'

'Death?' Kimberley's words were shaken and laced with terror as she scanned the darkest corners of the room.

'Not Death, just the curious man you left shackled to a table.'

'John?'

'Oh, come on. You can't say you're surprised, all things considered!'

'I, you, they, it, can't...'

'Do you want me to come back when you're a little more awake?'

'Well, could you?' Kimberley felt ridiculous and was grateful for the darkness when John replied.

'Let me just see what space I've got in my diary for mental connections with curious psychology students.' There was an awkward silence for a moment and she imagined John flicking the pages of some invisible diary. 'Nope, shouldn't be a problem.

Except the fact I don't get to choose when I can do this. So now is probably the best time.'

'Where are you?'

'In solitary. The Warden was mildly upset with my performance, apparently.'

'But how are you talking to me, then?'

Moving along the window, Kimberley kept her back pressed against the cold glass. Reaching the wall, her fingers fumbled for the light switch.

'I'd prefer you didn't turn the light on.' It was too late. No sooner had he spoken, the apartment was bathed in bright light.

'Stop messing around. How did you escape?'

'I told you, I'm still in solitary. Deep in the bowels of this awful place.' John sighed as Kimberley scanned the room for any sign of him. 'You'll do well to find me in there.'

'How are you talking to me then?' Pinching herself, hoping she would suddenly wake up.

'Whatever connection we had from those memories has lingered. It's not something I'm used to, not something I've tried on my own and I don't know how long it will last, so we should be quick.'

'What do you want from me?'

Kimberley moved around the room, checking every recess and corner as John spoke, but his voice seemed to be coming from everywhere and yet nowhere. Checking the front door was still locked, she turned back and faced into the room, seeing her reflection in the glass of the expansive window. Still dressed in the same clothes, her hair was a mess and she realised she looked as bad as she felt. Pushing the thoughts aside, Kimberley focussed her attention on John's voice.

'I need you to come back tomorrow, ask to see me again.'

'Why would I do that?'

'Because of what you've seen.' John's voice was calm, his words sounding almost inviting. 'You can't say I haven't tickled your curiosity.'

'Whatever you did to me, I don't want any part of it again.'

'It's too late for that.' He corrected. 'I could see the curiosity in your eyes, the fact you fought with the idea you may believe me. That's why I took the chance to let you in.'

'And what if I didn't want to go in there? What if I didn't want to see any of that?'

'It's a little too late for that. And now you have been there, I need you to come back.'

'I don't want to see that again. I don't want to see that monster, that thing, ever again.'

Kimberley's eyes fell on the pad that had fallen to the floor and the crude sketch of the Ripper she had made. More than anything, she had focussed on the lifeless eyes and imposing figure that had moved like a living shadow before taking shape before her eyes. Even the memory sent a shudder down her spine, and she quickly ripped her attention away from the notepad.

'I said the same.' John's voice crackled as he spoke, as if there was interference affecting him. 'You left your paperwork behind and something there caused me great concern.'

'Your own file?'

'No, a newspaper cutting you had amongst the papers. I'm not sure what it had to do with why you came to the hospital, but I need to know more.'

The voice was fading, growing more distant as John continued to speak.

'I can't come back. Running away like that, I expect the warden has already spoken to the university.'

'You can try.' John's voice was barely above a whisper now. 'Please.'

'I'll do what I can.' Kimberley offered, but she got no reply. 'Are you still there?'

Unnerved by the feeling she was alone and somehow not, Kimberley remained against the door for some time before she dared to make her way back across to the chair by the window. Looking down at the pad, she picked it up and folded the pages over, once again hiding the crude drawing of the Ripper's silhouette. The topmost page was adorned with words and the image of the Raven's curious appearance.

Tracing her fingers across the hooked nose of the Raven's plague doctor mask, she realised how odd the whole appearance was. Somehow his clothing was already at odds with the Gothic Victorian surroundings and yet she couldn't picture a period in time where he would have fitted. It was as if someone had somehow plucked him from an alternative place, existing alongside the one he had been in before, and brought into this world.

'Oh, stop being so stupid.' Kimberley scorned herself and tossed the notepad down onto the chair. 'It's all just a bloody dream.'

Turning away from the panoramic window, Kimberley made her way up the narrow flight of steps leading up to the raised bedroom in the open-plan apartment. Throwing herself down on the bed, she spent a long time staring up at the ceiling before sleep once again took hold. Unlike before, her sleep was dreamless and most importantly, silent.

7

— . —

AGAINST BETTER JUDGEMENT

Morning broke, and even as she ate her breakfast, Kimberley had not made up her mind. Her sleep had been uneasy, and she had seen almost every hour pass by through the night until the dawn sunlight poured in through the window. Showering after her breakfast, she soon emerged from the bathroom and once again approached the expansive window. Painted in the warm morning glow of the sun, the city looked nothing like it had in the misty night air when she had arrived home. London had been her home for some years now, forsaking her rural roots to chase her research. She had always been on the move, yet this apartment was the longest she had stayed in one place over the last nine years.

Unplugging her phone from the kitchen worktop, she moved to rest against the back of the seat in front of the window. Knowing nobody could see her, dressed only in her dressing gown, she rested her elbows on the soft material and took a moment to think things through. All the while, she kept her attention out of the window, making sure her gaze did not drift to the notepad.

Mulling over all the possibilities, her fingers unlocked the phone, and she quickly scanned through her contacts until she found the one she wanted. Pausing for a moment, she made her decision and hit the *dial* button and put the phone onto speaker. In a matter of seconds, the phone was ringing and after a half-dozen rings, a familiar voice answered the call.

'Miss Mansfield, I must say I'm surprised.'

'Warden.' Kimberley offered, blushing despite being alone in her apartment. 'I need to apologise for yesterday. It wasn't very professional and...'

'You're right, I would have expected such childish behaviour from a first-year student. Not one from someone with your level of experience.' Kimberley felt uncomfortable and knew this call was as much about damage control as it was about finding out what had happened the day before.

Deep down, Kimberley knew the damage such a foolish reaction could have. Not only in her career, but in her position and research. Having decided to contact the warden, she was doing it more out of self-preservation than to appease John, but deep down she had an insatiable curiosity about what had happened.

'That patient, John, he just unnerved me. It's not something I'm used to doing, I've never reacted that way before.'

'I know.' The warden's harsh voice interjected. 'I've spoken with your professor and your behaviour quite astounded him.'

Knowing she was definitely on dangerous ground, Kimberley was quick to allay any concern from the warden. Having only spoken to the woman via conference calls, never having met her in person, she was familiar with the warden's stern nature.

'I would like to pick up where I left off, if you'd be willing to give me a second chance?'

Leaving the question unanswered for an uncomfortable amount of time, Kimberley knew the warden was toying with her. In all of their correspondence leading up to her arriving at the Nuthall Hospital, she had picked up on the warden's need to assert her authority. Ever the playful hunter, Kimberley had met her fair share of people in similar positions and knew the personalities that came with the territory. Even her professor, a timid and quiet man, had warned her about the types of people who found their lives surrounded by delicate minds.

'I don't think a second visit with Mr Smith would be advisable.'

'On the contrary,' Kimberley quickly interrupted. 'I'd like to finish what I started with him. I think he was starting to open up to me.'

'A man like John Smith is nothing but a manipulator. Giving you access to him was a mistake, and not one I am keen to make again.'

Kimberley weighed up her options on how to tackle the tensions between them. Appreciating the warden's temperament, she knew the woman was testing her.

'If I'm not mistaken, the agreement between the university and the hospital gave me access to any prisoners who were category matches for my research. John Smith is one of those candidates and I'm sure the ethics committee wouldn't be too happy if I had to change venues at the last minute.'

'A change brought about by your childishness.' The warden snapped back.

Kimberley let her warning linger for a moment, knowing the warden would be seething at the sudden change of tact from her. That said, she also knew it was a calculated risk that had the potential to appeal to the warden's nature. After what felt like an age, the warden offered a curt and simple answer to her threat.

'John will be ready for you in an hour. I suggest you get moving. I've already affected the daily routine of my patients.'

The call ended abruptly, and Kimberley dropped it down onto the seat in front of her. Sighing to herself, she buried her head into her arms and took a few moments to compose herself before making her move to get dressed and head out to the hospital.

***

By the time Kimberley had navigated the morning rush hour and arrived at the grand gates of the Nuthall Hospitals, she had convinced herself the warden would not be there to greet her.

Walking to the gates, she pressed the call button on the post beside the gates and waited for it to ring.

'Welcome back.' The familiar gruff voice of the orderly crackled over the speaker. 'Use the side gate.'

Hearing the lock open, Kimberley pushed on the pedestrian gate and made sure it was secured behind her. Knowing she was being watched by the cameras mounted on every face of the hospital walls, Kimberley took a deep breath in and walked towards the expansive steps leading to the main doors. Climbing the sweeping stairs, she reached the door and stepped into the familiar reception of the hospital.

'The warden has asked me to escort you down.' The orderly announced through the speaker as Kimberley emptied her pockets into a plastic tray and placed it on the conveyor belt.

'Will I be able to speak with her?' Kimberley pressed as she stepped into the airlock scanner.

'I doubt it. I'm not sure she's in the mood, all things considered.'

Waiting for the door to open, Kimberley felt all eyes on her as the scanner made its slow pass over her body. Once the scan was complete, the glass door rotated open, and she stepped out to retrieve her belongings.

'Where are the papers I left behind yesterday?' Kimberley asked as she scooped her belongings and quickly followed behind the orderly who had already set off.

'They're waiting for you in the interview room.'

'Can I ask something?'

'You're the type who would ask, even if I said no.'

The orderly's less than welcoming manner caught her by surprise. Although she had known that her challenge of the warden's authority would have left her isolated from the stern woman, she had not expected it to resonate with the staff. Not wanting to appear unphased by the cold answers, Kimberley pressed as she followed along the winding corridors and into the elevator overlooking *The Deck*.

'How long has John been here?'

'What does it say in his file?'

'Were you here when he arrived?'

'He was a patient when I started. I've only been here for six, no, seven years.' The orderly offered as they reached the ground floor and the doors opened. 'John hasn't been in the general population at all since I arrived.'

'Why's that?'

'He has a way of upsetting people.' The orderly unlocked the doors to the older wing. 'As you learned yesterday.'

'Has he done that to other people too, then?'

'How other patients react to one another isn't really an easy way to assess how they affect people. Damaged minds affected by other damaged minds is hardly a stable assessment.'

'Why wasn't that in his files?'

'There's a lot that won't be held in the files the warden has shared with you.' The orderly stopped at the same interview cell she had been in the day before. 'That's your job now. To fill in the gaps by talking to him.'

'Are you going to be watching again?' Kimberley pressed as he unlocked the door.

'What? In case you decide to run out again?' Offering her a knowing smirk, he pulled the door open and stepped aside. 'If you could gather your paperwork up before you run away this time, please.'

Doing her best not to bite at the orderly's jibes, she offered him a dismissive glare and stepped into the room. As soon as she had passed over the threshold, the door slammed shut behind her and she focussed her attention on John. Bruises showing on his face, he offered her a wry smile as she drank in his battered appearance.

'What did they do to you?'

'Oh, what, these?' John chuckled and moved his hands in front of his face.

In the split second, his hands had covered his face, the bruises had disappeared and he once again looked fresher faced and playful. Offer her a coy wink, he motioned for her to take a seat on the other side of the table. Unlike before, his hands were shackled tighter, his movements were restricted, and he could barely reach to touch the table.

'How did you do that?'

'Parlour tricks. It gives the bully boys out there some reward for their brutish behaviour.' John quipped. 'Besides, I can hardly bruise when my icy heart hasn't beat in over a hundred years now, can I?'

'About that.'

'Please don't say you're going to sit there and pretend it wasn't real.'

'It's just, well, you know?'

'Please, can we accept the fact I shared a more than intimate memory with you? And, not to mention, spoke to you while you were in bed.'

'So it was you and not just some dream?' Despite the question, Kimberley had known it was John and was not a figment of a cloudy imagination.

Rising an eyebrow, John stared at her across the table. For the longest time, his hands in the smaller cuffs that help them almost palm to palm. 'Anyway, I've got questions about that news headline.'

'What about it?' Kimberley peered over the table but refused to reach for the cutting. 'It's just something I was considering looking into.'

'Pretty convenient, wouldn't you say?'

'How so?'

'After what you saw yesterday, I'm sure you can see why the headline piqued my attention.'

'It's just a glorifying headline, designed to sell more newspapers.'

'What about the crimes? Do they match the Ripper I showed you?' John's playful nature had evaporated and for a moment, Kimberley saw the intensity in his face she had seen when he had been resurrected as the Raven.

'I don't know too much about it.'

'You're lying.'

'I beg your pardon,' Kimberley stammered as her gaze shifted to the camera in the corner of the room.

'I can see it in your eyes. When you've been around as long as I have, you get a sense for these things. So please, don't insult me.'

'I'm sorry. I only know what's been reported in the news.'

'And?'

'They're saying it's a copycat of Jack The Ripper. Yes, their crimes are similar.'

'In which case, my hibernation in here is over.' John locked gazes with her and said his next words with great care, except his lips didn't move and she heard only his voice in her head. 'I need you to help me escape.'

'Not a chance.

'Keep calm.' Still, John's lips did not move. 'I won't ask anything more from you than to release me from these restraints. We will do the rest.'

'I'm not sure I can do that.' Kimberley was trembling as she spoke, her voice hushed to avoid the orderly hearing what she was saying. 'It would cost me my career.'

'I'll make it look like you weren't involved. You saw what that thing did in London.'

'I thought you killed it.' Kimberley protested.

'Clearly not.' John held out his hands towards her. 'Now please, you know what we have to do.'

Unsure of what to do, Kimberley perched uneasily on the edge of her seat. Knowing the eyes of the orderly, and most likely the warden, were transfixed on the camera feed from the room, she didn't know what she could do.

'Please.' John pressed, this time his lips moving with the words he spoke.

8

— · —

THE RAVEN

The aged Victorian wing of the Nuthall Hospital was eerily quiet. Within the corridor outside the interview cell, it was devoid of staff or any signs of life. The orderly observation station was along the length of the brick-lined passage and out of the way. Unloved and somewhat left on a slow journey to decay, it seemed fitting they had left John and a select few other inmates in that part of the building. Despite its age, the facilities were still secure and relied less on technology and more on the brutish security of brick and steel.

Despite the eerie silence, the door of the interview cell shuddered on its hinges. As dust fell from the brickwork, the orderly burst into the corridor from the observation room and looked towards the secured door. Again, the door shuddered, and the orderly launched along the corridor in response. As he reached the door, the metal frame exploded out of the wall, sending him crashing back into a cloud of dust and debris.

As the dust dissipated, the dazed man brushed off the mortar that had landed on his torso and stared wide-eyed as a silhouetted figure emerged through the jagged opening. At first the shape appeared distorted, somehow human, and yet not. What emerged from the cloud of billowing dust was not a man, it was the figure of a man, it was *The Raven*.

Once again, wearing the long black coat and plague doctor mask, John emerged through the dust and dominated the corridor.

'What the hell are you?' The orderly stammered as he scrambled on all fours through the debris.

'Sometimes the most unbelievable stories are true.' John declared, his voice muffled by the mask. 'Maybe next time you should take a moment to consider the truth behind the madness.'

'Smith?'

'No. The Raven.'

Turning his back on the orderly, his coat billowed behind him dramatically. Taking two steps, he heard the racking of the extendable baton and turned to look back at the young man. Unable to show his expression, John tilted his head to one side curiously and waited for the inevitable attack. Raising the baton, the orderly was fighting against the surge of fear as the metal weapon shook in his hand.

'You're not going anywhere.'

'I wouldn't waste your time.' John dismissed and turned away.

The attack came and, much to the orderly's dismay, the racked baton collided with the Raven's back and stopped dead in its tracks. Unflinching, he rotated on the spot and grabbed the metal bar, pulling the orderly closer. Only able to see his own reflecting in the large lenses of the mask's eyes, the orderly fumbled with his words as the Raven looked down at him.

'You...you...'

'Don't waste your breath.' John landed a solid blow on the other man's temple and allowed his unconscious body to slump to the ground. 'You don't know how long I've waited to do that.'

Discarding the now bent baton, John stalked along the corridor, leaving the unconscious orderly and a stunned Kimberley in his wake. Bursting through the doors into the new wing and out into *The Deck*, the sudden harsh light caught him by surprise. Emerging into the vast open space, he made it halfway towards the glass lift shaft before the air was filled with the sound of a blaring siren.

'Whatever this theatrical display is about, it ends now.' The warden's voice echoed in the vast space from the speakers mounted on the walls. 'I thought we were past all this, John.'

'It's time for me to leave.' John declared to the open air. 'I'd appreciate you making that as easy as possible.'

'We both know that's not going to happen.'

Standing in the middle of the room, he realised someone had already secured away the other inmates in their rooms. Turning around, the sound of speedy footfalls stole his attention from behind an imposing set of secured doors. Bracing himself, John cast his glance skyward and towards the skylight high above.

After a few long seconds, the doors burst open and a dozen armour-clad men marched in file into the room.

Dressed in blue coveralls and armoured in public order padding, they looked like police officers preparing for a riot. Fanning out, they formed into an extended line behind a barrier of transparent shields. Stretching the width of the room, they formed a solid barrier between John and his route out of the hospital. Rattling their batons on the front of the shields, the room became a cacophony of pounding as a half-dozen armed men took positions behind the shields.

Armed with stun guns and pistols, John knew he was in for a fight. The fact he had been hiding in the withering shell of his human form, the sudden opportunity to reconnect with his powers sent a buzz of excitement coursing through him.

'You don't want to do this.' John warned as he shrugged off the heavy black coat and removed the pair of escrima sticks from his back.

Testing the weight of his familiar weapons, John dropped into a defensive stance and prepared himself for the fight. In unison, the line of shields marched towards him. Biding his time, John watched the space between them close, all the while watching the wandering armed guards behind the line of shields. When the first shield got within striking distance, John made his move.

Dropping his weight into his legs, John launched up into the air and dived over the line of shields to land on the sterile floor behind the advancing line. Reacting as quickly as they could beneath their protective clothing, John disarmed the two nearest guards and sending them flying across the room. Making quick work of two more, the air was filled with the *crackle* of electricity as one of the armed guards fired their stun gun.

Feeling the barbs bite into his skin, John's body immediately locked up, and he fell to the ground writhing as the circuit sent his muscles into contraction.

'Get on him.' One of the guards screamed.

Feeling the weight of bodies diving on top of him, John was powerless against the waves of electricity immobilising him. Losing any view of the room beneath the sea of armour-clad bodies, John felt the relentless impact of blows as the guards set about doing their best to restrain him.

'I've got his hands.' Another voice screamed in panic.

'Get the cuffs.'

Mind racing, knowing if they succeeded in restraining him, his escape attempt would be over. John tried to calm his screaming mind but the flurry of confusion from his spasming muscles filled his brain.

'Move out of the way.'

As one of the guards adjusted their position to give them access to handcuff John, they managed to disconnect one of the probes from his leg and, in an instant, all sensation returned to his body. Not wasting time to celebrate the sudden return of his senses, John took full advantage of the change in circumstances. Finding footing, John pushed up and broke free from the heavy weight of the guards piling on top of him.

Sending bodies flying in all directions, John took a deep breath and watched as the world moved in slow motion around him. To him, the world moved in slow motion while to the world he moved with impossible speed. Ducking beneath a laboured punch thrown by the nearest guard, John delivered a solid upper-cut to the man's chin, lifting him into the air and ripping the Nato helmet from his head.

Moving to his next victim, John disarmed the man, ripping the self-loading pistol from his grasp as a round exploded from the short muzzle. Ignoring the projectile, John slammed his elbow into the next guarding sending a spider-web of cracks across the helmet visor. Moving along the line, John dispatched five of the guards before the disregarded bullet sank into his shoulder.

As the round bit into his skin, his momentum was lost and everything once again moved at normal speed. The five guards he had dealt with were now out of the equation and, to his dismay, the nearest two were armed with pistols. Firing a handful of rounds, John felt each of them find their mark in different parts of his body. Being dead had its advantages. Despite ripping through his torso and organs, the bullets could do no damage. Being nothing more than a distracting inconvenience that had halted his speedy attacks, John backed away until the two guards' magazines were empty.

'Waste of bullets, wouldn't you say?' John jibed as he admired the holes in his clothes.

As the guards instinctively reloaded, John attacked and immediately disarmed them. Snatching the top-slide from both weapons, both men looked on in horror as John grabbed the closest of the two and launched up into the air towards the enormous skylight high above. Crashing through the glass, the guard shrieked in terror as the remaining armed guards opened fire and John landed on the other side of the shattered reinforced glass.

Wind whipping around them, John span around and held the guard over the hole he had created in the glass. With the guard in the way, the firing from below stopped and John was able to speak with his hostage.

'What are you?' The guard stammered as John pulled the helmet off the man's head.

The guard was only in his early twenties and despite everything, John felt a wave of guilt at the terror on the young man's face. Taking a moment, John removed the plague doctor mask from his head and felt the cool breeze on his face.

'I'm the thing you've ignored and kept locked in the basement for too long.' John took a moment to savour the chilled air and the impressive view of London from atop the hospital building. 'I am Death's hand.'

'Don't kill me.' The young guard pleaded, balancing precariously on the shattered glass.

'Kill you?' John smirked. 'I'm here to protect you. Well, until Death requires your attention.'

'When's that going to be?'

'Not today!' John hushed and dropped the guard to the side of the gaping hole in the skylight.

Leaving the cowering man on the roof, John sauntered to the edge of the roof and looked down at the city below. It had been a while and yet the familiarity of the capital was still there. Searching the skyline, John saw Tower Bridge in the distance and a wry smile appeared on his face as he replaced the plague doctor mask on his head. Securing the leather straps in place, John turned his head to the sun and drank in his newfound freedom.

'Are you even with me these days?' John asked the empty space to his side.

Getting no answer, not honestly expecting one, John balanced on the edge of the roof. Hearing nothing but the roar of traffic below, John turned back to face the guard, who was delicately crawling away from the jagged hole in the skylight.

'Where are you going to go?' The man hollered as he clambered to safety.

'Back to my perch, watching over you all.'

As he finished his declaration, John leaned back, flipped into the air and over the edge of the roof. Allowing gravity to take its hold on him, John tumbled towards the ground and revelled in the excitement he had not felt in a long time.

By the time the guard reached the precarious ledge, there was no sign of John anywhere to be seen. Rolling onto his back, the guard stared up towards the moody clouds and allowed the tears of fear to roll down his cheeks.

What John left behind was a stark warning that he had been caged for too long. A fact he was not prepared to let happen again.

The Raven was once again free to honour his oath.

9

IN THE WAKE OF DAMAGE

Kimberley emerged from the cell after the sirens had stopped. Tentatively making her way back towards *The Deck*, she gasped at the sight that greeted her.

Bruised and battered, the armour-clad guards were in the process of collecting up the broken and discarded equipment. Catching the gaze of a bloodied guard whose helmet hung cracked on his belt, the man glared at her with contempt. The right side of his face was already swollen, the bruising showing across his cheek and eye-socket.

'Miss Mansfield.' The familiarity of the warden's voice sent a chill down her spine.

Looking around, Kimberley caught sight of the suited warden standing on the far side of the room. Hair swept back in a tight ponytail, her tailored grey suit added to the coldness she had become accustomed too. Following the warden's gaze, Kimberley couldn't help but gasp again as she saw the jagged hole in the glass skylight many levels above them.

'How did that happen?' Kimberley hushed as she made her way through the flow of recovering guards.

'I would expect you are well aware of how.' The warden snapped back, dismissing one of the guards from her side. 'Care to explain how my patient has escaped and you seem untouched, and unphased, by it all?'

Knowing the warden's suspicions would be levelled at her, Kimberley steeled herself as she made her way to stand in front of the middle-aged woman. Holding the warden's gaze, Kimberley suppressed the nervousness that coursed through her and waited for the inevitable interrogation that would follow.

'I don't know what happened,' She lied. 'One minute we were sat talking, and the next, he...changed.'

'Changed?'

'It's hard to explain.'

'Try.'

Knowing the truth about what had happened, Kimberley was able to sell her disbelief with absolute confidence. Having been seated across from John, the moment he had become the Raven had been a truly terrifying sight to behold. Seated across from him at the table, John had done nothing more than close his eyes and uttered a handful of words she could not make out. Whatever language they were spoken in, they were like nothing she had heard before. As he had finished speaking, Kimberley had watched the plague mask grow over his face, as if it had been there all along and somehow been invisible.

Rising from the table as the flowing black coat had materialised over his body, the chains of his restraints had fallen to the floor. Once everything had changed about his outward appearance, he had placed both hands on the table and leaned across the gap between them. His muffled words still echoed in her mind as she replayed the events in her memory.

'You'd do well to step aside. I have no intention of hurting you. In fact, I'd quite like to see you again.'

As soon as he she had moved aside, John, the Raven, had moved to the door and made his dramatic escape. Casting one last look back at her as the billowing dust exploded around him, Kimberley knew beneath the leather and metal mask he was smiling.

'Well?' The warden interrupted, snatching her back from her memory. 'What can you tell me?'

'The man that left that room was not John Smith. The man that left that room, well, I don't think it was a man.'

'You have been nothing but a problem. Come with me.' The warden snapped as she turned on her heels and stalked towards the open lift doors.

'This wasn't my fault.' Kimberley protested as she followed behind the warden.

Stepping into the lift, the older woman slammed a clenched fist into the control panel and waited for the doors to close as Kimberley fidgeted by her side. Once the doors had closed, the warden turned on Kimberley and towered over her, pressing her back into the corner of the lift. Terrified by the sudden coldness and aggression, Kimberley tried not to shake as the lift climb upwards and the older woman glared down at her.

'In twenty-four hours, you've set my team back in John's treatment program. What's more than that is the fact you've allowed him to escape.'

'I didn't allow anything.' Kimberley defended but fell silent from adding anything further.

'Whatever you did, and I know you did something, it has cost the reputation of my establishment. That is something that I cannot and will not accept.' The lift took an age to reach the upper levels and Kimberley felt relief as it ground to a halt. 'You'll forgive me if I rescind your open invitation to return for your research.'

Snatching the visitor label from her top, the warden snapped the printed plastic and allowed it to drop to the floor. Moving aside, she beckoned for Kimberley to leave the lift and rather than argue, Kimberley stepped out into the corridor in silence. With the warden stalking behind her, she guided Kimberley through the corridors and to a large room she had never been to before.

Reaching an imposing frosted-glass door, the warden barged past and thrust open the door before stepping into her modern office. Motioning with her hand for Kimberley to follow her, she moved to her seat behind a large black oak table and dropped down into it. Resting her elbows on the table, her demeanour changed as she rested her head in both hands and let out a long sigh.

'I'm sorry.' The warden eventually conceded as she pointed for Kimberley to sit. 'I know this isn't your fault. You have to understand the inquiries that will follow. It's just, I've spent my whole career building order from chaos and in a single day it's all come crashing down.'

There was sadness in her voice as she spoke, and Kimberley couldn't help but feel a sense of guilt. The stern warden had, in the matter of a few seconds, changed from the imposing figure to something akin to a broken woman. Sensing it was the fact they were no longer under the scrutiny of her employees, Kimberley sat quietly and waited to see what would happen.

'You'll need to be part of the investigation into how this happened,' The warden explained as she leaned back in the luxurious seat, her expression somewhat softer now. 'I don't expect it will be a speedy process.'

'I'll help in any way I can.'

'I know you will.'

'What will happen now?' Kimberley quizzed, as the warden reached for a crystal decanter from beside the desk and poured herself a long draw of whiskey.

'I've already reported the escape to the board. They've advised we are best dealing with it internally.'

'Hold on, don't the authorities need alerting?'

'As I explained before. We aren't behest of the national health service, we are equal parts private, and public funded. It gives us autonomy over internal matters.'

'So who will investigate any of this?'

'The board have their own processes.'

'Sounds a bit questionable.'

'Don't confuse my concern for weakness.' The warden interjected, catching herself before reverting to her aggressive and dominating nature. 'We will compile the necessary reports for the authorities, but we will keep this matter contained. At the request of the governing bodies.'

'And who exactly are they, the governing body?'

Feeling the warden's gaze on her, Kimberley looked around the room and admired the plethora of certificates and qualifications lining the walls. A large painting dominated the wall behind the desk, an abstract picture that appeared to show a crescent moon rising at an awkward angle. Sensing the warden's attention on her, Kimberley lowered her gaze and watched the woman take a long sip from her glass.

'It's probably better I don't prepare you for any questions. It would hardly be impartial if you knew everything about the function and workings of my hospital.'

'Agreed.' Kimberley conceded, not in any way believing what she was saying. 'So when does this all begin?'

'Our priority will be locating and apprehending John Smith. The investigation team will be supplementary to that.'

'So, what am I supposed to do?'

'We will be in touch.'

Leaving Kimberley hanging, the warden did nothing to dismiss her. Instead, she simply turned her chair around and faced the strange painting on the wall. Not wanting to overstay her welcome, Kimberley rose from the chair and moved towards the door.

'By the way.' The warden offered with a wave of her hand, still keeping the chair facing away. 'I will have your paperwork delivered to you, once we've gone through the contents. As part of the investigation of course.'

'Whatever you like.' Kimberley huffed and yanked the door open.

Navigating the interior of the hospital, Kimberley passed through the security gates and emerged into the early afternoon sun. Taking a moment at the top of the steps to the hospital, she couldn't help shake the feeling she was being watched. Turning her attention to the vast pale frontage, she caught sight of the warden standing by the glass of her office window looking down at her. Feeling the older woman's steely gaze, Kimberley pulled her coat tighter around her and hastily descended the sweeping steps.

Only when she was far from the Nuthall Hospital did she find a place to stop. Finding herself in a small public park, Kimberley found an empty bench and dropped down heavily onto the damp wood. As soon as she sat, she allowed herself to show her true feelings about what had just happened.

Having fought to suppress her fear and emotion, Kimberley had worn her mask of confidence as best she could. Fighting to keep the tremble from her hands, she had been relieved when the warden had dismissed her. Knowing full well the woman would not trust a word she was saying, Kimberley had made sure she was alone before allowing her a moment of release.

As tears streamed down her face, Kimberley looked at her shaking hands and felt a sense of dread and fear as she turned her gaze up towards the moody sky.

'What have I done?' Kimberley sobbed as she sat back on the bench, allowing her head to roll back. 'How could I have been so bloody stupid?'

Kimberley remained on the bench for some time before she felt the soft patter of raindrops on her face. Forcing herself to move, Kimberley gathered herself together and made her way back to her apartment. Moving through the growing crowds of shoppers, tourists and workers, she was grateful for the anonimity the busy city gave her. Despite seeing nothing, Kimberley was sure she was being followed but by the time she reached her station on the underground, she no longer had the inclination or energy to take a longer or more convoluted route to show out anyone who might be following her.

Knowing, if the warden had sent them, they would know her home address she decided the safest option was to go about her business. Acting in any other way would risk making her look suspicious. Opting for the safest course of action, Kimberley returned home and was relieved to lock the door and secure it from the inside.

Turning away from the door, Kimberley leaned against it and slowly slid down to sit on the carpeted floor. Looking across the open-plan apartment, she was about to move when a sudden voice spoke from the far corner of the room.

'I thought you'd never come home.'

Appearing from behind the dividing wall between the elevated bedroom and the rest of the apartment, Kimberley gasped as John leaned against the low wall. Still wearing the long black coat, he removed the plague doctor mask from his face and offered her a wry smile as he looked down at her.

'How the hell did you get in here?'

'Is that all you can think to ask?'

'Get out.' Kimberley boomed as she stood up. 'If they catch you here, I'm done for. I've done my part, now please leave.'

In the blink of an eye, John disappeared from the bedroom space and reappeared standing in front of Kimberley. Gasping at the sudden teleportation, Kimberley backed against the door and stared wide-eyed at John.

'How?'

'Shall we talk, or should I just leave?'

Kimberley ripped the door open and step aside, giving John a clear path into the hallway.

'You can leave.' She didn't meet his gaze but her voice was firm.

Taking his leave, John walked past her and offered one last hushed comment as he brushed past her.

'You're already involved, more than you know. You'll know where to find me, when you change your mind.'

10

— · —

A FAMILIAR CRIME SCENE

London looked different than John remembered. In the thirty years since he had arrived at the Nuthall Hospital, a lot had changed, not least of all the people that meandered the busy streets. Needing to be away from the crowds, John now found himself perched on the edge of Nelson's Column overlooking Trafalgar Square. Silhouetted by the bright exterior of the National Gallery, he remained obscured by the shadows created by the spotlights directed at the infamous statue behind him.

In his guise as The Raven, John was able to remain hidden from view and had watched the dying sun set behind the skyline of impressive buildings. Surrounded by the more traditional London buildings he remembered from his past, John somehow felt more at home here than he did amongst the crowds below. Watching the evening play out, John remained perched on the edge of the marble platform until the moon had risen high into the night sky.

'Not what it used to be, wouldn't you say?'

Once again John looked around, somehow hoping that Death would answer him from the heavy shadows cast by Nelson's statue. Getting no reply, John removed the mask from his face and admired it in the moonlight. Having been unable to manifest himself as The Raven, it had been a long time since he had admired the intricate design of the leather mask.

Tracing his fingers around the shimmering lenses, he brought the mask closer to admire the fine embossed detailing that covered each face of the plague doctor mask. moving along the length of the curved nose, his fingers reached the metal embossed tip of the beak and he felt the cold metal against his fingertips.

'How long has it been since I wore this?' He quizzed himself as he turned over the mask. 'It still feels the same when it's on my face.'

Bringing the mask closer, John was about to the replace it on his face but stopped short as the moonlight caught the inside of the plague mask. Something caught his eye that he had not noticed before. Rising to his feet, he moved around the platform until he was bathed in the bright light of the spotlights mounted at the base of the statue.

'An oath. An honour. Death's hand in human form.' John read aloud the sentences etched into the metal rim of the right lens.

In all the years wearing the mask, he had never noticed the lettering and had a sneaking suspicion it had not always been there. Inspecting the inside of the mask for anything else he had not noticed before, he found nothing. Feeling the frustration building inside him, John once again looked beyond the statue and the silhouetted skyline of buildings that surrounded him.

'Death's hand. So where the hell are you?'

Scrunching the leather mask in his hand, John stepped to the edge and allowed the mask to fall from his grip. Tumbling to the ground far below, John watched until he could no longer see it falling. Lifting his attention from the people below, John knew he needed a purpose, knew he needed to find the reason he had felt the desire to leave the confines of the hospital. Despite having found peace within the confines of the walls, there had always been something itching inside him and having seen the newspaper clipping, John knew it had something to do with the headline.

Once again removing the crumpled paper from his pocket, John read the headline and the article once again. All the while, his attention was drawn to the word **RIPPER** that seemed to almost call to him from the page. While Kimberley had dismissed the article as a typical sensationalist headliner, there was something in his instincts that told John this was something more.

'Fine!' John huffed as he replaced the cutting in his pocket. 'If I'm ever going to get some peace, I need to see what this has to do with me.'

Looking down at the ground far below, John offered a wry smile and took his leap of faith out into the air.

Seated on the raised plinth of the infamous column, two young students sat drinking and talking. Oblivious to all that was happening above them, they had not noticed the discarded plague doctor mask tumble to the ground behind them. Engrossed in their conversation, neither had any awareness of what was happening until John crashed into the stone platform right behind them.

Landing with a sickening *crunch*, both of them screamed as John's lifeless body came to rest at an awkward angle on the pale stone. Confused by what had happened, the two strangers backed away from John's body, wide-eyed and stammering to find their words.

'How'd he get there?' One of them eventually mustered.

'Must have jumped.'

'What, from up there?'

'We should check if he's alive.'

'Go on then, you check him.' Pushing his friend forward, the other was caught by surprise and offered a scowl.

Inching closer, the young man looked down at John's face and the fact his eyes were still open. Leaning closer, he held a shaking hand over John's mouth and felt no warm breath against his skin.

'Damn, I think he's dead.'

'Is there any blood?'

Dropping to his knees, the man reached out to check beneath John's head for any blood when the impossible happened. As his fingertips brushed John's hair, he turned to look at the man leaning over him.

'As nice as that may be, mind if I get up?' Knowing terror would freeze the man, John couldn't help but smile as he sat up.

Unable to move, the young man's mouth opened and closed as he fought to find his voice to scream. Cracking his neck and shoulders, John felt his bones return to their proper positions. When his body had recovered from the sudden impact, John rose to his feet and looked down at the young man who remained on his knees with his mouth opening and closing comically.

'Could you pass me that?' John asked as he straightened the collar of his coat, pointing out the discarded mask by the kneeling man's side. 'Probably shouldn't have let it go like that.'

Dumbfounded by what was happening, the young man picked up the mask and held it up for John to take. Offering a courteous smile, John took it and replaced it on his head. Once the leather straps were secured, he pulled up the hood of his coat and took a moment to compose himself. Knowing he was still finding his connection to the powers Death had given him, he was in a delicate transition back to himself.

'You'd do well not to tell anyone about any of this.' he offered, his voice muffled by the mask. 'I can't imagine people would believe it and, trust me, you don't want to look like you belong in a mental hospital.'

Before either of the young man could reply, John launched himself off the stone base and disappeared into the night. Leaving both of them dumbstruck by what had just happened. How a man had crashed into the stone base and simply brushed it off, was beyond comprehension.

Wasting no time in the fact he had found enough connection to his powers, John moved through the London streets like a spectre in the night. Unseen by anyone, he moved at an impossible speed through the streets, leaving nothing behind but a dark vapour trail along the path he had come. Having stalked the shadows of London for decades, John knew exactly where he needed to go and how he was going to get there.

In a matter of seconds, he had made it halfway across the capital and allowed his journey to end as he entered Whitechapel.

Allowing his racing senses to settle, John realised he was in Buck's Row, but the street sign now read Durward Street. Taking in his surroundings, John realised how much had changed and yet he sensed the familiarity of his newfound surroundings. Turning in the middle of the cobbled street, John's attention was drawn to the flashing blue lights of a police van and solitary officer in a high-visibility jacket at the far end of the road.

Removing the mask and allowing his appearance to change and match his surroundings, John approached the tired constable that leant against the bonnet of the idling van.

'Can't go down this way, mate.' The grumpy officer waved as John approached.

'What's happened here?'

'You kidding? Been all over the news.' The young policeman muttered. 'You ain't some reporter, are you?'

'No, I've been away for a while.'

Thrusting a leaflet into John's hand, the policeman turned away and opened the door to sit inside the police van. Turning away from the secured crime scene, John read the information leaflet the officer had given him. John's heart sank as he read through the warning leaflet that detailed the fact police had discovered a young woman's body in the early hours of the morning and were appealing for witnesses. Sensing death in the air, John ensured he was out of the police officer's view before he once again became The Raven and transported himself into the alley beyond the crime scene tape that fluttered in the gentle breeze.

Stepping into the shadows of the alleyway, John looked around and felt his heart sink as he saw the splatters of blood that had sprayed across the brickwork. Relieved to see they had removed the body, there were enough indications of where the young woman had died to draw him to the right place. Closing his eyes, John felt his mind wander back into what had happened in the dreary alleyway.

In his mind, he saw the victim, a young woman no older than Kimberley, entering the alley and finding her way blocked by an imposing figure at the far end. Silhouetted by the streetlight, the enormous figure stepped into the flickering light and John ripped his eyes open and turned to face where the figure had been.

'It can't be.' John gasped as he realised the figure that had blocked the alley was none other than the Ripper.

Needing to escape the confines of the alleyway, John burst from the shadows and ran through the fluttering of police tape to the surprise of the officer in the van. Unable to react, the policeman screamed after him as John disappeared into the anonymity of the night.

Having escaped knowing something was unbalanced in the world, John had hoped his instincts had been wrong. Having seen the murder scene and vision of the past, he now knew the Ripper had indeed returned and it was his duty to honour the oath he had made to Death.

A forgotten sentinel.

Recruited by Death.

To protect humanity from evil.

His escape had simply returned him to his duty.

EPISODE

11

FREEDOM

11

— • —

REUNITED

'STop where you are, asshole!' The voice was ragged, struggling to catch his breath as he shouted.

John moved with grace as he dived over a set of railings and dropped down fifty-feet to the pavement below. Launching from the balcony of the apartment on the banks of the Thames, John landed with grace and turned to look up to where he had come. Seeing the burly figure bound onto the balcony, John smiled as he saw the look of confusion on the man's face.

'Hey, you!' The man pointed a finger at him. 'How'd you do that? Stay there.'

'Not a chance.' John quipped as he waited for the man to return into the apartment before disappearing into the steady flow of people around him.

The advantage John had with his powers included his ability to deflect people's attention from him when it was needed. Much like diving three storeys from a balcony and landing unharmed on the ground, John knew it was best to shield his movements from curious eyes. Of course, their brains would sense something, but by the time their eyes registered the impulses to look, he would be invisible to the conscious mind.

In truth, the most dangerous witnesses were the ones who did not realise what they were seeing. As John stalked along the embankment of the walkway, he recalled a time when his presence had been seen and even reported by a witness. Where the conscious mind could be fooled, a less controlled mind could not be so easily deceived. The young man that had seen him, back in the eighties, had been riding the waves of a heroin trip, and so his mind was already clouded by the drugs that raced through his system. To this day, John could not recall what he had been doing in his guise as the Raven, but he knew the man had seen him.

Although able to distract the minds of those around him, it was a skill that took a lot of attention and concentration. For that reason, it was something that John would do in fleeting moments. That was the reason he was happy to portray a visible face to the world as John Smith and shield himself only as the Raven and only when it was absolutely necessary.

Hearing the frantic scream of frustration, John chanced a glance behind him and smiled as the burly man scanned the crowds for any sign of John.

'Find what you were looking for?'

The voice stopped John dead in his tracks and before he could respond, a pair of hands dragged him into a narrow alley that sat between two buildings. Away from the crowds, John was about to call the presence of the Raven to him when he realised the voice belonged to Kimberley. Releasing a long sigh of relief, John offered a smile and leant himself back against the wall behind him.

'I'm surprised to see you here.' John quipped as he took in her appearance.

'So am I.'

'How did you know where I was? Signed yourself up for the fan club, have you?' The playful smile quickly disappeared as Kimberley frowned at his playful retort. 'Oh come now, surely you can't always be that serious?'

'I wasn't, until I met you!' Kimberley groaned as she looked back at the crowds of oblivious people only a few feet away. 'Now it seems you're haunting my dreams.'

'I promise that's just a side effect and not some supernatural way of me stalking you.' Again, the playfulness was wasted.

'I can't shake the images you showed me at the Nuthall, it's like they're etched inside my head.' John realised how tired Kimberley looked and felt a pang of guilt as he looked at her. 'I tried to find you after you left my apartment, but I didn't know where to start.'

'So, how did you find me? It's a pretty unlikely coincidence you bumped into me walking down the street.'

'No, I followed you here, obviously.' Kimberley quipped. 'I found you yesterday when you left the old warehouse in Whitechapel.'

'Whose a clever girl then?'

'Shove it!' Kimberley bit, frustrated by his flippant reply. 'I only knew you'd be there because...'

'Yes?'

'Because all I've seen for the last few nights are snapshot images of the murders you saw.'

'Oh.'

'Exactly.' Kimberley's eyes welled with tears as she replayed the haunting grizzly images in her mind. 'I've never had to think about things like that before. Don't get me wrong I've researched the sort of people who were held in the Nuthall Hospital, but these were memories. They felt so vivid.'

Pushing away from the wall, John used his gloved hand to wipe the tears from her cheeks.

'They are memories, and I expect the emotions are with them too.' Kimberley could only nod as she avoided looking up at him. 'I can only say I'm sorry for showing them to you.'

'You made me see them?'

'Well, not exactly, but I know there was a chance you would be tarnished by the memories from our connection at the hospital.'

'Can you get rid of them?' It was John's turn to fidget uncomfortably at the question. 'I thought not.'

'Listen, this isn't the place to be talking about this. We should get out of public view and I can help ease your mind and answer some questions you have.'

'Forgive me for not trusting you. I'll settle for a cafe somewhere, but I'm not going to some derelict warehouse with you.'

'Fair enough.' The playful smile returned to John's face. 'A coffee date it is then, Miss Kimberley Mansfield.'

Offering her his arm, Kimberley was disarmed by his sudden change in demeanour and pushed him away. The disturbing memories were forgotten for a moment as they emerged back into the flow of pedestrians along the embankment. Scanning the crowds, John felt relief as he saw no sign of the burly man and quickly guided Kimberley away from the apartment block and away from the Thames.

Before long, the pair had found a small cafe in the heart of Soho and far enough away from the hustle and bustle of London to talk in confidence. Although the shop was alive with the steady stream of people, positioned by the window in the corner, they were left alone to keep their hushed conversations private.

'Are you sure you don't want something to eat?' Kimberley pressed as she set about eating an oversized muffin.

'It's a waste, my dear. These long-dead tastebuds make food a somewhat pointless affair.'

'Don't you eat at all?'

'What's the need? I've been dead for over a hundred years.' John leant back and took a sip of tea.

'And that?' Kimberley scoffed as she bit into the muffin. 'Surely you can't taste that either, can you?'

'Certainly not, but what's an Englishman without a cup of tea?' Once again, John offered a disarming smile as he sipped from the large mug.

'So, tell me, what were you doing back there?'

For a moment, John hesitated with his answer. Scanning around the interior of the cafe, he made sure there were no eyes on him before finally removing a sheet of parchment from his pocket. Placing it onto the table, John pushed it across to Kimberley and waited for her to look at the sheet.

'What's this?'

'I was searching for information about the Ripper, about his crimes in your modern world.'

'And you found this?'

'Not exactly.'

Kimberley wiped her hands before unfolding the parchment and stretched it out on the table between them. The paper was thick and discoloured, yet the text and images were crystal clear, as if they had only just been written. On the left side of the sheet, a large horned demon's head dominated the page while someone had filled the rest of the page with hand-written text she could not read.

'What is it?'

'The man who had it, I found him hiding in the shadows of the warehouse, looking for me. I followed him and wanted to find out more.' Tapping the sheet with his finger. 'And that is what I found.'

'I'd expect he works for the hospital. I'm aware that the warden is trying to keep your escape secret.'

'They've probably got a tail on you too. I'd not be surprised if you've not led them to me.' Despite the comment, John seemed far too relaxed. 'Then again, I'd expect they'd have stormed the place by now if they were here.'

'So, what is this?'

'Back when I was working the Ripper case, before I became this, I saw something similar on the Inspector's desk. I only caught a glimpse of it and was told it was a line of investigation for the higher ranks and not a lowly constable like me.'

'Is this the Ripper?'

'I believe it is.' John mused. 'The fact that man had this tells me he isn't anything to do with the hospital.'

'So why was he following you?'

'There are others in this world who know of my existence, and the existence of the Ripper. I believe he is one of them.'

'Didn't you ask him?'

'It wasn't really the time.' Taking back the page, John refolded it and slipped it back into his jacket. 'Are you sure I can't convince you to join me in the warehouse? I promise I'll try my best not to murder you.'

'Don't joke. You forget, I only met you a few days ago, and you were an inmate at a high security hospital.'

'Well, you read my file, did it say anything about being a killer in there?'

'You know it didn't. But it also said you weren't some undead supernatural creature.'

'Well, that's one way to put it I suppose.' John was somewhat deflated by the matter-of-fact nature of Kimberley's response.

'So, considering you sought me out, do I take that as a sign you're willing to get involved in this curious world of mine?'

'I don't think I'm left with much of a choice, other than going mad with the things you left in my head.'

'In which case I'll need you to trust me.' John's demeanour changed as he fixed his attention on something outside the cafe window.

'What's wrong?'

'You're going to meet me here.' John slid a folded napkin across to her. 'Remember the address and destroy it before you leave. I'll draw them away and you make sure you're not followed.'

'Followed by who?'

'The warden and anyone else she's sent.'

Rising from his seat, Kimberley watched as John once again transformed into the Raven. Unseen by anyone else, Kimberley had expected shocked gasps, but there was no recognition that any of the patrons had seen anything.

'What are you going to do?'

'Distract them.'

The world seemed to move in slow motion as Kimberley watched the Raven move. Launching himself from the table, his long coat billowed behind him as he dived towards the glass window at the front of the cafe. Expecting to see the glass shatter, it dumbfounded Kimberley as the Raven passed through the glass and landed on the pavement outside. Turning his plague doctor-masked face to look at her, had she seen his face

Kimberley knew he would have offered her a cheeky wink as he launched out into the street and *over* a van that moved at a snail's pace in the slow-motion world around them.

'This is mad,' Kimberley groaned as she watched him disappear behind the van. 'What have I got myself into?'

12

— · —

THE REVENANT

J ohn had sensed them before he had seen them. While he had been talking to Kimberley, something had caught his attention through the window. At first he had disregarded it as his old senses coming back to him after all those years confined within the dark bowels of the Nuthall, and then it had moved. Seeing the aura of death, John was sure his raven's eyes had become attuned to the movement of the dead.

Seeing nothing untoward in the street, John scanned wider until his gaze fell on a curious figure on the rooftop of the opposite building. Silhouetted by the heavy sky, there was no mistaking the faint smoke that drifted in the wind. Dressed in all black, the figure looked human, but John had known it was not.

His movement through the window had once again gone unseen by the inattentive masses, and only Kimberley had seen his spectacular departure from the cafe. Pleased by the fact she was seeing him in his true form, John had launched over the van in the road and set about searching out the Revenant he had spotted on the rooftop.

Moving with grace, John scaled the front of the building and landed on the roof's edge with his coat settling behind him. Scanning the now vacant rooftop, he pulled out the pair of escrima sticks as he dropped onto the roof from the ledge.

'There's no point in hiding.' John warned as he stalked the length of the empty roof. 'I know you're here.'

'You saw,' the voice replied somewhere to his side. 'Yet you do not see me.'

Snatching his masked head around, John saw nothing but felt the Revenant's attack as a solid blow crashed into the side of his face, sending him crashing to the ground. Rolling over his shoulder to soften the fall, John dug his heels into the stones on the roof and skidded to a stop a short distance from where he had been standing. Seeing nothing, he realised his skills were still unreliable and while he knew the Revenant was there; he was unable to see it.

Another attack landed, this time finding its mark on his chest, once again sending him crashing to the floor.

'You're hardly the sentinel they warned me about.' The invisible voice mocked as it moved for another attack.

Sensing the movement, John drove his weapons up and out away from him and felt satisfaction as they found their mark. Moving on instinct rather than anything else, he moved around and drove the escrima stick in his right hand over and down to be met with a satisfying *crunch*. As his unseen opponent crashed down, it finally came into view.

Laid on the roof, dressed in tight-fitting black clothes, was a Revenant, an undead creature that was all too familiar to him. Twisted and part-decomposed, the resurrected souls of the undead were trained to seek out creatures like the Raven that existed in the place between life and death. Discoloured skin and dead eyes looked up at him as the Revenant removed the tattered cloth that had been covering its face. Had John not been expecting it, the sight of the lipless mouth and discoloured bones would have surprised him. Having seen it before, his instinct was to fight and not shy away from the devilish creature.

'Nice to see one of your kind again.' John mocked as he shrugged off his coat and let it drop to his feet. 'I've been without an opponent worthy of my attention for quite some time.'

'This isn't a game.' The revenant spat as it rolled away and righted itself.

Moving as it did, the undead creature folded itself up and over backwards, sprawling its arms at impossible angles until it stood tall a short distance away. Rotating its dislocated shoulder back into position, it offered the Raven a cocked head as an invitation to fight.

'It may not be a game to you.' John remarked as he tested the escrima sticks in his hands. 'But to me, you're the warm-up after many years of resting.'

Not offering any more words, John launched himself towards the Revenant. Deflecting the attack, the two of them fought across the length and breadth of the rooftop. More than once, the slippery Revenant used its grotesque ability to contort its body to avoid an attack or parry. Twisting itself underneath and around John, the Revenant succeeded in gripping both John's wrists and pulling them away from his body at awkward angles.

'You've certainly lost your prowess.' The Revenant hissed, its mouth hovering close to the Raven's mask.

'Just warming up.'

Dropping his weight, a quick shift of balance was enough to break free of his opponent's grip and John pushed away to find himself disarmed in the process. Seeing the Revenant toss the escrima sticks over the edge of the roof, John clenched both fists and set himself in a defensive stance. Having used the weapons to keep the undead creature at bay, John knew the fight was about to get much more personal. Having seen the Revenant's ability to rotate and distend its joints, John knew this was not the best method of attack, but there was little he could do about it.

Using a sturdy aerial as a launch platform, the Revenant climbed the pole before launching itself up and over in the air to hammer down its attack on John. Overpowered by the attack, John struggled to keep his guard as the Revenant ducked and dodged around him, using its flexibility to its advantage. Blow after blow crashed into his mask and soon, John was struggling to keep his attention fixed on the impossibly fast creature.

More by luck than skill, a wayward fist crashed into the Revenant's stomach as it lunged forward. Stopped dead in its tracks, John heard the sickening sound as his fist broke through the flesh contained within the tight-fitting clothes. Recoiling in disgust, John had enough of a distraction to turn the tables in his favour. Choosing to drop his weight, John launched an uppercut through the air and felt satisfaction as his fist collided with the Revenant's jaw.

Dislodging the lower jaw, the creature let out a startled yelp as the force of the impact ripped the toothy jaw from its position and sent it clattering to the floor. With a sickening tongue lolling around as it moved, John wasted no time in following the attack with another. In a handful of heartbeats, had there been any between the pair of them, John turned the tables in his favour. As his last attack took the Revenant's legs from beneath it, John scooped himself around and took hold of the creature's neck.

Snatching it from where it was standing, John hoisted it over the ledge of the roof and held it in the air.

'Care to explain who sent you to find me?'

'What are you going to do? Drop me! We both know that will do nothing.' The words were hard to distinguish as it formed them without the lower jaw being in place.

'I have my ways.'

With a wave of his hand, John created a small section of swirling black smoke immediately behind the Revenant's head. Twisting the decaying monster to see the smoke, there was a moment of realisation as its face hovered close to the swirling smoke.

'You wouldn't.' The creature pleaded as blood, and drool dribbled from its face and down John's gloved hand.

'I bloody well would.' Pointing his free hand towards the discarded lower jaw, the bone flew through the air to land in his open hand. 'Here, that should loosen your tongue a little.'

Without a care, John rammed the jaw back into position. Given the opportunity, the Revenant securely hooked it back into place and tested its movement. To anyone observing, not that they could, it would have been something comical to see the dangling creature re-affixing its face together. Despite the comedy of the action, the moment was serious and sombre.

'You will get nothing from me.'

'You know what that is, right?'

'Yes.'

'And we both know despite all the dark magic that holds you together in this world, you'll never recover from that.'

'Do your worst.'

'Seriously?' John hissed and ripped the plague doctor mask from his face. 'You're going to make me do this?'

They both knew he was prepared to. The steely cold look in his eyes told the Revenant as much, but it knew better than to talk. Without waiting for an answer, John pushed the hanging creature further out over the ledge and pressed its face into the swirling smoke. A shrill scream of pain filled the air and in response a flock of pigeons burst from their nesting boxes on the adjacent roof.

'Enough!' The Revenant screamed, but John kept the creature held where it was.

'This is the only way you bastards feel anything.' John snarled as he watched the smoke press into the creature's face. 'Now, are you prepared to talk?'

Pulling the Revenant back, he allowed it to explore the side of its face that was now missing. Where John had pressed the creature into the smoke, whatever it was had devoured the rotten flesh from its face and left nothing but pearly bone in its wake.

'You know who sent me.'

'The warden?'

'She seeks to have you back.'

'And she would use you?'

'The Society offered our services to help find you.'

'Our?' The realisation dawned on John that the Revenant was not alone.

Hearing footsteps behind him, John was slow to react. Still holding the Revenant in his hand, he turned to greet the new arrival and stopped in his tracks at what he saw.

Instead of another black-clad undead monster, it was Kimberley who had made her way to the rooftop. Looking at him, eyes-wide and mouth moving silently, John cursed under his breath.

'What, what...' Kimberley stammered and struggled to form a sentence.

'This thing is a Revenant.' John answered as he turned back to the creature. 'I was about to let it go, but I can't do that now.'

'Why not?'

'Because it's seen you. They'll know you were with me.'

John's demeanour changed as he hooked the plague doctor mask back over his face. Ever theatrical, John moved his arm back out and pressed the Revenant towards the swirling smoke again. Distracted by Kimberley's arrival, John had missed the creature's subtle movements. As John moved his arm back out, the Revenant ripped a jagged dagger from its back and whipped the blade through the air.

Surprised by the attack, John staggered back and released his grip on the creature. Landing on the ledge, it thrust out with the weapon again, allowing the blade to leave a deep gouge in the leather mask on his face.

'Oh, what fun this will be.' The creature pointed the knife in Kimberley's direction. 'I'll be seeing you again.'

Lunging forward one last time, the Revenant used the distraction and launched itself off over the roof's ledge. Dropping to the street below, there was no sign of the creature as John reached the side to look down.

'Bugger, that's a problem!'

'What did it mean? It'll see me again?'

'Well, you won't be able to return home now. The warden sent that thing to find me, and now she knows you're with me.'

'Wait, the warden sent that thing? You mean she knows all about this?'

'Of course she knew, I told her.' Kimberley struggled to comprehend what she was being told. 'It was part of the original agreement for me being locked away, but that story is for another day. We should go.'

'Wait just a minute. You're telling me she sent a, well, what was that?'

'That's a Revenant. Think of it is a sort of bloodhound or sniffer dog, trained to pick up the scent of those of us who exist on the plain between life and death.'

'But still, the warden has one of them?'

'Not exactly.' John tensed as he was about to speak. Something deep in his senses sent a trickle of fear coursing through him. 'We should go. Now!'

Not waiting for an answer, John surged forward and took Kimberley's arm.

'Wait just a minute.'

'Do you trust me?'

'What?'

'Do you trust me?' John was running now, dragging Kimberley towards the opposite side of the roof.

'No.'

'Oh well.' Reaching the ledge, John stepped up and jumped off the roof, dragging Kimberley over the edge with him

13

— • —

THE RAVEN'S SAFE PLACE

Creeping through the deserted warehouse, John made sure the building was clear before he ushered Kimberley in through the concealed entrance.

'Not much, I know.' He quipped as he slid the metal sheeting back into place behind them. 'But it's all I could find on the market right now.'

'How can you keep joking about things?' Kimberley snapped as she looked around at the dreary derelict building.

'Trust me, when you've been couped up in a cell for thirty-odd years, you find ways to amuse yourself.'

Stalking past her, John dodged the debris strewn around the open warehouse and made a beeline for a door on the far side of the building. Hearing the pigeons coo in the rafters, he was glad his senses could not identify the odour of the building. Judging by the look on Kimberley's face, it was something akin to the smell of Victorian London that was somehow still lodged in his memory.

'Why this place?' Kimberley quizzed as she slipped on a particularly concentrated pool of pigeon mess.

'It's central to where I need to be.' John explained as they reached the door. 'I have a feeling the Ripper won't stray far from his hunting ground.'

'Whitechapel isn't what it used to be, it's changed.' Kimberley explained as she watched him unlock the door. 'There are other places in London where he could find the same type of victims.'

'Ladies of the night, you mean?'

'That, and other things.'

'Well, perhaps you can school me in this new world of vice and disarray. Seems I've missed a lot since I've been locked away.'

'Where are you taking me?'

'To my secret lair, the home of the infamous Raven. Protector of humanity, scourge of evil.' John offered a dramatic bow as he ripped open the door. 'Or else it's just an old vault where the rats haven't crapped in and I get some peace and quiet.'

Seeing the deflated look on Kimberley's face, he was certain she was about to storm off when she broke out into laughter. The sudden amusement caught him by surprise and hearing her laugh echo in the rafters made John feel somehow human, if only for a moment. Casting aside the thought, John descended the dark staircase and soon faced the heavy, reinforced door of the abandoned safe.

'What sort of place has a safe like this underneath it?' Kimberley gasped as she admired the enormous door.

Like something out of a film, the cylindrical vault was bathed in flickering light as John flicked the crude switch by the open door. Allowing their eyes to settle, Kimberley drank in the curious interior of the vault. Newspaper cuttings and maps lined one wall while the other housed a small cot bed and a collection of curious items she could not place.

'Back in my day, it was an old mill house, but I've no idea why this is here.'

'You've been busy.' Kimberley hushed as she stepped over the threshold and moved to look at the newspaper cuttings. 'It's only been, what, three days?'

'Four.' John chuckled as he looked at the leaflet the police officer had given him at the crime scene. 'And I don't have the time to waste when I've got the warden looking out for me.'

'And those Revenant things?'

'Same thing.' John mused as he ripped one clipping from the wall and handed it to Kimberley. 'This one. What can you tell me about it?'

'I saw it in the newspapers. It's the one the clipping was about that you found in the interview room.' Kimberley looked closer at the array of clippings. 'Not all of these are about the new murders, are they?'

'No.' John moved along the wall to a collection of older clippings. 'These are copies of the reports from the last time.'

'Can I ask something?' Kimberley placed the leaflet on a pile of boxes and looked at her host. 'If you're saying you defeated this Ripper thing, how has it come back?'

'Now, that's something I'm still trying to figure out.' John croaked, a lump forming in his throat. 'Clearly I have a lot to answer for.'

'What do you mean by that?'

Dropping onto the makeshift bed, John shrugged off his coat and offered out his hands to Kimberley. Even without words, she understood the offer and what it meant. Although she was curious, the offer of once again returning to John's memories was equal parts inviting as it was terrifying. Seeing John sat on the makeshift bed, he looked nothing like the masked fighter that had burst out of the cell. To anyone else, John looked like nothing more than a homeless man who had found his solitude in an abandoned warehouse.

'I can show you again, if you like.'

'I'm still trying to undo the mess you left behind the last time.' Kimberley snapped as she turned her attention back to the clippings. 'Going back really isn't something I'm keen on doing again.'

'I can explain it, if you'd prefer. But I'm not sure you'll be able to see what I want you to.'

'I'm listening.'

Taking a seat perched on a wooden crate, Kimberley waited for John to begin his explanation. She watched him as his eyes scanned the wall beside her and at last settled on a particular article.

'I remember the first time they sent me to guard one of the Ripper's crime scenes.' The rings around John's eyes appeared darker in the flickering light of the vault. 'It was Mary Ann Nichols, and it's a scene that I'll never forget. I suppose it somehow put me on the path to this.'

Manifesting the plague doctor mask in his hands. Admiring the gothic mask, he saw his own reflection in the eyepieces. The face that looked back wasn't what he remembered. Despite being the same face, there was something else behind the exterior and he realised the mask of the Raven had become as much him as the physical appearance he carried.

'That's the same place as the latest murder, isn't it? I remember reading it and thinking whoever this copycat was used the location to make a statement and claim his nickname.'

'What they released in the newspapers wasn't everything. Even more so back then, the media were strictly controlled. The stories started out well-curated and it was only in the later murders when the frenzy took hold that the powers that be lost control.'

'What didn't they release?' Kimberley's curiosity was piqued.

Rising from the bed, John moved to her and hung the plague doctor mask from one of the open doors on the wall.

'Back in my times, there weren't as many cameras pointing. it was easier to hide the visual evidence.' Inching his hands closer, he knew Kimberley could see his movement, but she did not pull away. 'Despite the fact the only images of the actual scene are locked in the archives, I can still see them in my memory as clear as day.'

John's fingertips hovered over Kimberley's hands but it was her who made the final move. Pressing her hands to his, Kimberley closed her eyes as she once again felt herself dragged from her seat on the crate and into the dark world of John's mind. Feeling the sensation of being swallowed by an enormous wave, all her senses closed down. Desperate to take in a lungful of air, Kimberley found her lungs unwilling to respond. Feeling the rising panic, she no longer felt her hands brushing against John's fingers.

'Open your eyes.' John hushed in her ear, his voice telling her he was hovering right beside her.

Calming her racing mind, Kimberley opened her eyes and waited for the world to come into focus around her. Kimberley found herself once again standing in Victorian London. Despite everything, even knowing this was a vision, the world around her was so visceral. Taking a moment to absorb her surroundings, Kimberley was grateful the smells were missing. Judging by the steady flow of fluids down the channels in the pathways, she expected the smell would not have been pleasant. What she could experience, on the other hand, was the sounds of Victorian London nightlife.

'Where are we now?'

'This is the night I was sent to Mary's body.'

On cue, the younger version of John appeared around the corner wearing the same uniform as before. Scanning the dark alleys and street, younger John looked troubled and walked with a heavy weight on his shoulders. Smoothing over his collar, John moved along the street and found his way blocked by a burly man.

'Mind your step.' John scorned as he bounced off the powerful physique of the drunken stranger.

'Mind yours, copper!'

'I said mind your step, now move.' Even from a distance, Kimberley could see John's confidence was feigned. Luckily, the drunkard did not.

'Or else what?'

John moved with surprising speed as he drew his wooden truncheon and had it pressed to the burly man's neck in a heartbeat. Pushing the larger man back, John pushed hard until the man gagged at the pressure on his neck.

'Or else you'll find your last pound paying for a surgeon to fix your face.'

Nose-to-nose, the drunken man was about to speak again, but John took the wind from him with a solid knee to the crotch. Stepping back, John let the man slide down the wall and end up in the foetal position with his legs soaked in the flowing refuge in the gutter. Offering a curt nod, John replaced the truncheon in its holder and continued along, leaving the gasping man in the gutter.

'We should follow him, me.'

Falling into place behind the younger memory of himself, John guided them through the back streets of Whitechapel until they reached a hive of activity. A handful of people were being held back at the entrance to a narrow alley.

'Make way.' John's memory declared as he pushed from the back of the crowd. 'Clear a way or you'll find yourself in a cell for the night.'

As the reluctant crowd parted for the new arrival, Kimberley and John caught sight of a familiar face. Ahead of the crowd, the Inspector that John had spoken to in the earlier memory stood leaning against a wooden fence smoking. Seeing the man, Kimberley felt the need to hear the inevitable conversation and pushed past her guide in hot pursuit of the younger memory.

'Where are you going?' John snapped as the crowd started to close in around them. 'You're not supposed to make waves.'

'What do you mean, make waves?'

Bumping into a portly woman, Kimberley was about to offer her apologies when the woman shrieked in terror. Eyes wide, the colour drained from the woman's face as she looked directly at Kimberley.

'It's fine, I'm...' John clasped a hand over Kimberley's mouth and moved her away from the terrified woman.

Much to Kimberley's surprise, the woman's eyes did not follow their movement but remained transfixed on the spot where she had just been standing. Careful not to disturb any of the others in the crowd, John guided Kimberley in his memory's wake and felt relief as they reached the front of the gathering and followed into the shielded entrance to the alley.

'What was that all about?' Kimberley snapped as she pulled John's hand from her mouth. 'They're just memories.'

'Memories that can turn on you in an instant.' John confessed as he saw Inspector Abberline guide his younger self deeper into the shadows. 'We are trespassing in my subconscious, cause too many disturbances and the memories will become hostile.'

'What do you mean by hostile?'

'You've seen what I am capable of, my transformation into the Raven and the powers it gives me?'

'So?'

'This is John's mind. The Raven's is a much darker and more dangerous place. Consider us two sides of the same coin, balanced and yet opposed. These memories have not been corrupted by the Raven's yet. Cause too much of a disturbance and this world of memories will soon see us as the enemy.'

'This is messed up!' Kimberley declared as she looked to the still frozen woman in the crowd. 'Why can't anything about this be easy, or bloody well normal?'

'I don't think you can make taking a trip into an undead man's memories any more normal than this.' Once again it was John's wit that defused the simmering tension between them.

'Should we follow them?' Kimberley pressed as John's memory and the Inspector disappeared around a corner.

Answering with an outstretched hand, they sat off behind the two policemen.

14

GOING BACK

'You shouldn't be in such a rush.' John warned as the two men ahead of them stopped. 'What you're going to see is something that has haunted me for a long time.'

'Is she down there?' Kimberley felt her heart skip a beat in her chest. The idea that a murdered woman's body lay just around the corner filled her with dread.

'Yes. But you should listen to them first.'

Turning his attention to John, he subconsciously mouthed the conversation word for word as his younger self and the infamous Inspector conversed in the shadows. Although he struggled to hear their voices, John knew the exact content of the conversation. He had watched it over and over in his mind when the only solace they had given him in the Nuthall Hospital was the sanctuary of his own memories. Watching Kimberley inch closer, suddenly nervous at her own presence in the world of John's subconscious, John couldn't help but smile.

'Under no circumstances,' the voice carried from beyond the bend in the alley. 'Can anyone but my investigation team come down here. We can't have a mass panic.'

'Understood, sir.'

Following the path of the alleyway, John was close on Kimberley's heels as they emerged into a narrow courtyard. The body of a young woman had been draped with a white cloth that already showed the stains of blood from the hidden wounds. Feeling his eyes move to the corpse, John took a moment to compose himself. The sense of calm confidence disappeared for a second as he remembered the feelings of what was about to happen.

'You will speak of this to nobody.' Inspector Abberline commanded as he stalked across to the body. 'Is that understood?'

'Yes, sir.'

Both of them watched as the Inspector ushered the younger memory of John to the covered body. Crouching down, the Inspector took a long draw on his pipe as he gripped the bloodstained sheet in his shaking hand. Despite all his years and all the things he had seen, it was clear that this crime had unnerved the seasoned detective. Moving with more drama than he had intended, Abberline pulled the sheet back and revealed the mutilated corpse beneath.

Despite the amount of times John had replayed this memory, he still recoiled at the sight. Although he felt nothing now, the flurry of emotions that his younger self was feeling, were all too familiar.

'What monster did this?' He heard his younger self gasp.

'Monster indeed,' John scoffed as he looked across at Kimberley. 'How naïve I was, wouldn't you say?'

Completely engrossed by the disturbing sight of Mary Nichols' body on the cobblestone floor, Kimberley did not even react to John's voice. Unable to remove her eyes from the gluttony of grotesque injuries that covered Mary's torso, Kimberley stepped closer, trying to see more. To her disgust, Kimberley could see the tattered flesh and organs within the gaping cavity left behind by the Ripper. The sight that upset her the most, however, was the jagged wound that stretched across Mary's neck and the lifeless eyes that stared up at her in pure terror.

'Seen enough?' Abberline hissed as he draped the cloth back over the body. 'She will be transported to the mortuary by daybreak. I need you to remain here and ensure her body remains untouched.'

'I don't need to see this.' Kimberley protested as she turned to look at John. 'I hope you didn't bring me here just to show me that?'

'Not at all.' John protested as he guided her away from the hushed conversation between the two men. 'I brought you here to help me make sense of what is now and what is then. This is the same place as the murder a few nights ago, but something feels different.'

'I've not seen the scene of the other one.' Kimberley protested. 'And I don't want to either.'

'Come with me.'

Moving behind the talking men, John guided Kimberley to a small gated area to the side of the courtyard. Pushing the gate open, he offered her no invitation and descended three small steps into a small rear yard. Bathed in the flickering streetlight, John pointed towards the wall at the far end of the yard.

'What's this?'

'They'll find it in a minute, and you'll hear the conversation I had with Inspector Abberline. I thought it was useful for you to see this first, so you can listen to what we talked about.'

Allowing her eyes to adjust to the dim light of the yard, Kimberley could make out the vague outline painted on the wall. At first it looked like nothing more than lines and scribbles, but as her eyes adjusted, the details came into focus. Stepping back to the gate, Kimberley couldn't quite believe what she was saying.

'Is that, blood?'

'Yes.'

Painted in Mary Nichols' blood was an enormous effigy of what Kimberley recognised as a demon of some sort. Scrawled in a language she did not recognise were a series of letters and symbols in a circle around the demonic figure.

'What does it say?'

'The moon's protection provides me shadows to feed.' John sighed as he repeated the phrase verbatim as he had a thousand times before.

'And what does that mean?'

'I've never understood its meaning.'

As they spoke, Inspector Abberline appeared at the open gate behind Kimberley. Moving out of his way, not that he could see her, she watched as the Inspector guided the memory of John to the spot where she had been standing. As the inspector bathed the yard in light, Kimberley and John could see the dribbling blood staining the brickwork was till fresh.

'Is that in the killer's hand?' John's memory stammered as he drank in the image and symbols.

'I have an artist attending with haste before we remove it from the walls. I would see that done before daylight where all the neighbourhood can see it.'

'What are these symbols'

'I have no idea, but I have seen them before.'

'Where?'

'You're aware of the murder in December?'

'No, sir.'

'A woman's body was found in Commercial Road with horrific injuries. We had thought it an act of a disturbed mind until I saw this.' Abberline pointed to the effigy on the wall. 'The same symbols were painted in her blood on the doorstep, something we never released to the newspapers.'

'But that was nearly a year ago.'

'Yes, and there have been more.'

'ABBERLINE?' A stern voice hollered from the alley.

'Speak this to no-one.' Abberline warned as he stalked past the memory of John. 'I'm trusting you, because you're new and have no allegiance to others.'

'ABBERLINE!' The voice repeated.

Leaving the memory of John alone in the yard, Kimberley and John removed themselves and returned to find Abberline in a heated conversation with an older man of similar dress.

'What's that about?'

'From what I remember, he is Scotland Yard and very much on a different path than the Inspector.' John reminisced as his attention returned to the shrouded body. 'You must appreciate, in those times, it was all about who you knew. Inspector Abberline was a good man, I had been a project for him before my death. Perhaps he saw some promise in me.'

'What did he mean there were others before this? Even I know this was Jack the Ripper's first victim.'

'There have always been whispers and rumours, there were more. The problem with an urban legend like this will always be the rumours and elaboration. It's something you can never escape, and it makes it hard to trace back for clues. All I know is what Abberline told me.'

'But how does this help us now?'

On cue the world disintegrated around them and was replaced by a much more modern view of a similar alleyway. John could see the swimming disorientation in Kimberley and lurched forward as she collapsed.

'I've got you.' John soothed as he clicked his fingers and the memory faded away.

Returning into the vault, John launched from his perch and caught Kimberley as she repeated the motion of passing out as she had in the memory. Lowering her with care, John could see she was physically shaking and made sure Kimberley was comfortable before he ripped the blanket from the makeshift bed and wrapped it around her.

'Take a few minutes.' John hushed as she moved to leave the vault. 'I'll only be out there if you need me.'

Leaving his guest alone on the floor, John made his way through the open door and stepped out of view. Alone in the shadows of the basement, he cursed under his breath as he peered into the deep shadows beneath the staircase.

'Are you even there anymore?' John hissed. 'I know you were never at my beck and call, but come on. I'm here like a fool fumbling blindly in dark.'

He knew he would get no answer from Death. He could count on one hand the amount of times he had spoken with Azrael since the moment he had turned. Staring into the shadows, John longed for an answer, some encouragement to say he was on the right path. Having been severed from his connection to Death's gift while imprisoned in the Nuthall Hospital, it was a strange feeling to have all of his senses back under his control. Massaging his wrists unconsciously, John looked around and realised how strange it all seemed now.

'Thirty years can make a vast difference.' He hushed to himself as he looked at the decaying interior of the abandoned warehouse building. 'I'm just like this place. On the verge of ruin and standing with no sense of purpose anymore.'

John did not notice Kimberley's movements until she announced her arrival with a subtle cough. Smiling to himself that she had made him jump, John turned around to see her standing in the doorway with the blanket draped over her shoulders. Her face had drained of colour and she kept herself steady by leaning against the corroding metal door.

'Do you always talk to yourself?' Her voice was hoarse and quivering as she spoke.

'It's a habit you get into when you live like I do.' John confessed, releasing his wrists from his hands. 'I thought the solitude of the hospital would ease my mind. All it did was slow the flow of thoughts. I realise now I was foolish to give them the means to restrain me.'

'Is that why you couldn't escape on your own?'

'You remember the bracelets?' Kimberley nodded, hanging on his every word. 'They restrict my ability to use my powers. Sure I won't age, but the ability to move at speed or manifest as the Raven are stopped by them.'

'What are they made of?'

'That I don't know. I found them many years ago when I was trying to find my purpose. I gave them to the warden when i asked her to house me.'

'Why would you do that? Lock yourself away?'

'Look at it from the point of view of what I am and what I am capable of. Without a sense of purpose, I'm nothing more than the creatures that stalk the shadows.'

'But you said they feed on the living and you were there to stop them.'

'Yes, but when my need is no longer there and my death eludes me. What's more dangerous than the creature I am with nothing to do?'

'What can you do?'

John offered a smile as he dropped down to sit on the bottom steps. Taking a moment to compose an answer, he saw the look of eagerness on Kimberley's face. Despite the pale skin from her sudden removal from his memory, she still reminded him of a face he had thought forgotten.

'Azrael charged me to be his sentinel. As the name would suggest, I can fly and move in a way that seems fast to you.'

'Like you did at the hospital, that was impressive.'

'I find the slipstreams between life and death and move in them. Other than that, there's obviously the lack of ageing and eternal good looks.' John caressed his stubbled cheek as if showing off a hidden youth with a wry smile. 'You've experienced the ability to mine my memories.'

'Can you do that to other people?'

'Yes. But as you saw back then, we have to move with care, so we remain invisible to the host's consciousness. Of course, it's easier to control when the memories are my own. Entering someone else's mind, especially someone in a state of conflict or obstruction, creates a very volatile balancing act.'

'What happens if they find you?'

'The mind risks collapsing. In your profession, I'm sure you've seen minds that no longer function as you would expect.' John rose to his feet. 'Besides...'

A large clatter from the main warehouse cut his sentence short. Eyes wide, he glanced at Kimberley and motioned for her to return to the vault. Before she could protest, the face of a Revenant peered through the opening at the top of the stairs.

15

———

FIGHTING BACK

In a heartbeat, John dragged his hands over his head, calling the plague doctor mask and long coat to his body. Dropping into a fighting stance, John watched from behind the blue-tinted lenses of the mask as the Revenant dropped from the ceiling and appeared in its full form at the top of the stairs.

'You're not the one I met on the rooftop.' John snarled as he pointed a gloved finger up towards the new arrival.

'Oh, he's here too.' The Revenant declared menacingly as a second creature appeared at its side.

John saw the Revenant had tied a strip of discoloured fabric over its face to keep the snapped lower jaw in position. It also covered the exposed bone on the side of his face where John had thrust its head into the swirling smoke. Offering a smile, John waited for the inevitable attack to come.

'I see you're struggling to talk. Need a hand with that?' In response, the Revenant simply raised a fist and thrust its crooked middle finger up at John. 'Now that's a little rude.'

Clearly frustrated, the battered creature lurched forward and was quickly stopped by its companion. Trying to push past it, the accompanying creature whispered something in the other's ear which appeared to calm its attempts to lunge down the stairs towards John. Like a rabid dog straining against its lead, John eyed the pair with suspicion and waited for the inevitable attack.

'What do I do?' Kimberley hissed from the open vault.

'Stay in there. No matter what you hear, leave them to me.'

Lifting the hood of his heavy coat over his head, the plague doctor mask returned over his face as John once again took on the form of The Raven. Eyeing both the revenants through the blue-hued lenses, he waited to see how they would react. As the battered creature from the rooftop strained against its companion's restraint, he knew it best to make the first move. Not giving his opponents the time to formulate a plan, John launched up the staircase.

John landed on the top step, the heavy coat billowing like wings behind him and offering enough of a distraction to land the first blow. Driving a clenched fist upwards, he felt a wave of satisfaction as the injured Revenant was lifted into the air by the force of the blow. Using the momentum of his attack, John flipped himself over in the air and slammed his foot into the creature's face with a sickening *crunch*. Collapsing beneath the attack, John rolled over his shoulder and skidded to a stop on the dusty floor facing back towards the staircase.

'You move with surprising skill, considering you've been absent for so long.'

'You never lose it.' John smirked beneath the mask. 'You've got one chance to leave us be and go back to your master like the good dogs you are.'

Knowing the answer, John pulled the escrima sticks from his back and kept himself crouched low. Helping the injured Revenant to its feet, the two creatures turned their attention to John. Launching up into the lattice of metalwork that secured the corrugated roof, the injured Revenant disappeared amongst the shadows above like a skulking rat. Tracing its movement by the sound of bone on metal, John refused to relinquish his attention away from the second Revenant.

Eyeing the creature with suspicion, he sensed the movement from above as the other creature attacked. Working in unison, the other lurched forward as John adjusted his posture to deflect the attack. Unable to protect himself from both directions, John felt the solid blow and sting of pain as both Revenants lashed out. Using the claws on their hands as their only weapons, John heard the fabric of his coat tear and the sting of pain as the razor-sharp tips pierced his flesh.

Despite being devoid of life, John could still feel the burning sensation caused by the cursed creatures. Retracting himself back, John once again whipped the coat from his body and tossed it out towards the nearest of his opponents. Catching the Revenant by surprise, John launched into the air and crashed down on the blinded creature. The fight became much more furious as it fought to break free of the tangled clothing while fending off the flurry of attacks from John.

Once again, John manifested the swirling orb of smoke and light in the air and wasted no time in dragging the Revenant's arm towards it. Only at the last minute did the coat slide from its head, but by then it was too late. Unable to pull itself free, John dragged the Revenant's arm *through* the swirling orb and out through the other side.

At first, the revenant showed no reaction. That soon changed as the tendrils of smoke dissipated and John jumped back, allowing the severed arm to drop lifeless to the ground. Where the Revenant's arm had passed through the swirling smoke, the mottled flesh had been devoured by whatever dark magic had formed the orb, all that remained was the brittle bone that easily snapped as John released his grip.

Fuelled by anger and pain, the Revenant surged forward and released a blood-curdling scream as it moved.

Drawn by the sounds of fighting, Kimberley had crept from the safety of the vault and now peeked over the top step, keeping her profile low to remain unseen. Aware that the second Revenant was somewhere in the shadows of the warehouse ceiling, she was careful to remain hidden but found her attention stolen by the impossibly fast battle between John in his guise as the Raven, and the Revenant.

To John, his movements felt normal, unlaboured and precise, yet to Kimberley, her eyes struggled to keep up with the speed and momentum of their fight. John would move with impossible speed as he ducked down, around and over to deliver a solid blow at the Revenant. Dumbfounded by the fact John had cleanly severed the Revenant's arm through the strange ball of smoke, Kimberley backed away and felt her heart sink as she heard footsteps on the stairs behind her.

'Curious little girl?' The bandaged Revenant snarled as it snatched her from the ground.

The first John knew of Kimberley's capture was her shriek as the Revenant ripped her from the ground. Wrapping his arm around the Revenant's neck, John gripped the undamaged hand and yanked it back at an awkward angle until he heard the bone *crunch* in the socket.

'Stay where you are.' John warned, his voice muffled by the plague doctor mask.

'I care nothing for my brother.' The other Revenant mumbled as he pushed Kimberley ahead of him. 'Unlike your care for this, woman.'

'Lets not pretend you're not bothered.' John retorted as he forced the bone to press against the rotten flesh of the Revenant's shoulder. 'I know, as well as you do, the flow of your kind from down there isn't as frequent as it used to be. There can't be many of you left.'

'There's enough.' The creature in his arms spat. 'And what's to say the gates haven't opened while you have been hibernating in the shadows?'

'Because I doubt they would have sent dumb and dumber to face me if there were more of you out there.'

Frustrated by the veiled threat, John twisted the Revenant's arm just enough to split the discoloured flesh and expose the

ball-joint bone. Snarling to keep from screaming in pain, the
Revenant tried to bite at John's face but found his teeth gnash-
ing harmlessly in the air.

'That being so,' the other creature declared as it stalked closer,
keeping Kimberley ahead of it with his talon claws pressed into
the back of her neck. 'I stand by the fact you have more care for
her than I do for him!'

'You're probably right.' John conceded. 'So, what are we going to do from here?'

Scanning his surroundings, John's attention settled on a
jagged strut of metal that hung down from the ceiling at an
awkward angle. Years of abandonment had taken its toll on the
once impressive structure and what had once been a support
beam from the roof had become coroded and dislodged from its
anchor points. Making the mental calculations about trajectory
and position, John drowned out the incessant remarks from the
revenant and focussed his attention on what he planned to do.

'Are you listening to me?' The Revenant boomed as it pressed
its fingers into the flesh at the top of Kimberley's spine.

It was the yelp of pain that dragged John back from his
thoughts. As he snatched his attention back to Kimberley, he
was certain he saw movement in the darker shadows under the
roof, but had no time to look back. Seeing the look of pain on
Kimberley's face, he decided and acted. Pressing his knee into
the Revenant he still had hold of, John pulled back until the
creature's arm was dislocated from the socket. Releasing his grip

on the creature, he pushed it aside and once again Kimberley could see nothing of what happened next.

Casting the disabled Revenant aside, John allowed the world around him to slow and pressed towards the creature holding Kimberley hostage. Directing his movements to the right, John closed the gap between them in a heartbeat and planted himself on the Revenant's side. Seeing the creature's head move at a laboured speed to look at him, John smiled beneath the mask and launched himself up into the air.

Having positioned himself as he had, his movements dragged the creature away from Kimberley and propelled them both up into the air and towards the jagged strut of metal in the ceiling. Nearing the corroded metal, John twisted his body and watched with great satisfaction as the Revenant's torso collided with the razor-sharp rusted metal.

Cleaving the creature neatly in two, John watched the look of pain and terror on the creature's face as the metal passed almost completely through its lower torso. Landing on the roof, John planted his feet and stood upside down on the rooftop with the Revenant wedged against the metal in front of him. Releasing his control over the speed of time, John's hair dangled above his head as he turned his masked face towards his trapped opponent.

'Get me down from here.' The Revenant spat, its discoloured blood seeping from its mouth.

'Tell me why the warden has accepted the Society's help.'

'No.'

'Does she know how they intend to hunt me down? Does she know about your kind?'

'End it now, I'm not telling you anything.'

'Last chance!'

'End it.'

'As you wish.'

Seeing Kimberley looking up, John manifested a larger orb of swirling smoke in the air between them. Staring at the Revenant, he knew the creature would not betray its master. Knowing the futility of any further questions, John stepped to the trapped Revenant and slid it free from the jagged metal strut. Succumbing to the pull of gravity, John watched as the creature tumbled towards the swirling orb of smoke and passed through it.

Seeing it consumed by the orb, John dropped to the ground and landed across from Kimberley as the remains crashed to the ground between them. The mass of charred bones that landed on the ground bore no resemblance to the Revenant. Instead, it looked to be a mass of smouldering flesh and blackened bones topped with a skull whose lifeless eye-sockets now stared up at Kimberley.

'What did you do to it?' Kimberley stammered as she stared down at the mess on the ground.

'It's the only thing that works on those types of things.'

'And what is that exactly?' She pointed up to the swirling orb that collapsed in on itself and disappeared.

'I'll explain more, but we need to get moving.' As if on cue, the second Revenant crashed through the door on the far side of the warehouse and disappeared from view. 'He'll bring more with him.'

'Where are we going to go?'

'The only place I can think of.' John declared as he stalked back towards the vault. 'Back to the crime scene of this latest murder. Maybe we can find something there.'

'The police will not let you anywhere near that place.'

'I can be persuasive.'

'No!' Kimberley snapped, stopping John in his tracks.

Stalking to him, she took hold of the plague doctor mask and ripped it from his face. Surprised by the calm expression, and the almost comical lopsided grin, she dropped the mask to the floor.

'What?'

'You've got to promise me no more killing.'

'You expect me to leave Revenants to walk away?'

'No, I mean people, no more killing people.' John's flippant reply frustrated her. 'And you can wipe that stupid smile off your face. I won't go anywhere else with you unless you promise, no more killing people.'

'So you're happy to wander around on your own knowing they're after you?' John pointed to the still open door the Revenant had escaped through.

'Well, I...'

'I'm messing with you. No more killing the living, how's that?'

'Better. Besides, I didn't kill anyone at the hospital!'

'Really, the mess you made would have said different.'

'Trust me,' John offered his casual grin. 'They all lived to fight another day.'

Hearing sirens in the distance, they both tensed and silently agreed to make good their escape. In a matter of minutes, the warehouse was once again empty, save for the smouldering remains of the Revenant on the dusty floor.

16

— · —

THE FULL MOON SOCIETY

T he battered Revenant crashed into the crypt and collapsed on the ground. Sounds echoed around the vast
chamber, and the creature took a moment to orientate itself. An
enormous fire raged on the far side of the room and the bricked
walls were adorned with ornate carvings of demonic creatures.
Most of the figures could have been attached to church spires
and watched from the skies above, but within the crypt, they
looked like guardians, their hollow eyes scanning the vast space.

'You return alone?' A sinister voice snarled from in front of
the fire.

'My companion was ended by the Raven.'

The Revenant flinched at the sound of smashing glass as the
figure tossed a glass into the fireplace. The alcohol within ignited
the fire even more and gave enough distraction for the figure to
rise from the seat in front of the fire.

The crypt itself was a curious setup. Three large stone
coffins dominated the part of the room nearest to the revenant.
Adorned in a variety of unrecognisable symbols and images,

they seemed to be the focus of the vast room. The far side of the crypt was more akin to some study in a manor house or similar. Bookshelves lined the walls from floor to ceiling and a large table sat behind the trio of exuberant high-back chairs that faced into the enormous fireplace. It was the occupant of the centre chair that now turned their attention to the Revenant.

'Twice you have been bested by the Raven? How disappointing.'

Like a well-trained dog, the Revenant shuffled forward at the unspoken command of the imposing figure. Simply pointing a gloved finger to the ground at its feet, the figure waited for the battered Revenant to skulk its way across the crypt.

Bathed in the dancing light of the fire, the figure wore a well-tailored charcoal suit and a black mask covering their nose and mouth. As the Revenant neared the figure, the piercing blue eyes shimmered in the firelight and it was clear the figure belonged to a well-built and muscular man.

'He was more in tune with his powers than you led us to believe at this point.' The Revenant declared as it arrived at the man's feet.

'He has been contained within the hospital for three decades. His powers dampened and restrained, and yet he cast you both aside.'

'We would have been more prepared if you had...' The Revenant was silenced by a solid blow as the man swept the back of his hand across the demon's face.

'I'm not looking for excuses.'

Stunned into submissive silence, the Revenant watched as the man stalked past it and came to rest with both hands on the oak table behind the chairs. Taking a moment to compose himself, the man scanned the vast crypt and considered the sudden change in circumstances.

'Maybe the woman at the hospital wasn't truthful at the level at which they restricted his powers?' The revenant offered, checking its cheek where a jagged gouge had appeared from the man's blow.

'Why don't we ask her?'

Before the Revenant could respond, the doors opened to the crypt, and the warden was escorted into the room by two figures dressed in all black with their faces hidden behind balaclavas. Unperturbed by her surroundings, the warden offered a respectful nod of her head at the man standing on the far side of the table.

'You have a question of me?' Her words oozed with confidence as she stalked across the crypt.

'The Raven,' the revenant stammered. 'He was more powerful than he should have been. Are you certain he was restrained while in your charge?'

'Someone who knew every detail of his strengths gave the manner of his restraint to me. I am in no doubt they suppressed his powers.' She arrived at the table and placed a large silver coin on the wooden surface. 'You forget, my part is more than a simple hired guard.'

The warden slid the silver coin into the centre of the table and waited for it to settle. In response, the masked man did the same, producing his own coin from his jacket pocket and sliding it to meet the warden's in the middle. Each coin depicted a distinct face staring up towards the vaulted ceiling. The warden's was adorned with a triple-horned demon whose deep eyes stared upwards while the masked man's showed a larger demon with only a pair of crooked horns.

'That may be the case, but he was stronger.'

The masked man turned on the spot and closed down the Revenant in two strides. Taking hold of the creature's neck, he ripped the Revenant from where it crouched and thrown through the air to land on the oak table. Caught completely off-guard, the creature slammed into the solid wood and the warden was quick to act and pin both its arms to the tabletop.

'Two trained Revenants, bested by the shadow of a man.' The warden hissed in the creature's face as it struggled against her grip. 'We were misplaced to put our trust in you.'

'I did as I was asked.'

Overcome with panic, the Revenant lifted its head and watched in horror as the masked man sauntered back to the roaring fire. Silhouetted by the flames, the Revenant thrashed to break free, to no avail. Moving with almost theatrical speed, the masked man retrieved a thin-bladed sword from the fire and turned back to face the table. Seeing the red-hot metal of the blade, the warden's twisted smile filled with the panicking creature with dread.

'You failed to do as you were asked.' The man hushed as he moved back to the table. 'We do not release the minions of Descent simply to be a mere distraction. Not when we are so close to fulfilling the prophecy.'

'I did what I could.'

'And that wasn't enough.' The warden hissed in its ear. 'Your time of use to the Society is over.'

'No, I can do more.'

Writhing on the table, the Revenant's face was awash with panic. Hovering her face over the creature, the creature could see its own reflection in her cold eyes. Pressing the sizzling blade against the fabric tied around its head, the Revenant felt the heat against its blackened skin and froze where it was. Knowing any movement would bring the blade into contact with its face, the creature dared not move.

'You know this blade?' The man teased as the blade burned through the discoloured fabric.

'Yes.' The Revenant replied, its jaw dropping loose once he had cut the fabric free.

'This is the Master Blade, gifted by the Dark Angel of your dominion.'

'I know what it is.' The looseness of its damaged jaw muffled the Revenant's reply.

'Despite our every effort, you have failed to return the Raven to us. A failure that will not be replicated.'

'I can still be of use.'

'Yes you can.'

In one swift movement, the masked man drove the super-heated sword down through the air and severed the Revenant's arm. As it's piercing shriek filled the air, the warden released her grip and he delivered his second attack with impressive precision. Sitting bolt upright on the edge of the table, clutching for the stump left behind, the sword swept through the air and cleaved the Revenant's head from its shoulders in one.

Immediately the Revenant's body crashed to the tabletop and the warden moved back as the cauterised head rolled across the table towards her. Stopping it with her hand, the head came to rest with its lifeless eyes staring at her. Although the creature had already been dead, born of the afterlife and resurrected solely as their work hound, the dark skin now appeared ashen and empty.

'Place it in the fire.' The masked man barked as he dragged the headless corpse off the table. 'I would put it all to use, but it offers little sustenance for the prophecy. For that we need something with more life yet left in it.'

Obeying the snapped instruction, the warden lifted the head from the table and stalked across to the roaring fire. Taking one last look at the demonic creature's face, she realised how curious it looked. Although she had seen Revenants before, it had always been at a distance. Seeing the mottled flesh, it almost looked reptilian as she traced her fingers across the angular cheekbones. Knowing she was being watched by the masked man, she tossed the head into the flames and watched the darkened flesh ignite until the head was nothing more than a ball of fire.

Casting her attention to the stone arch that contained the fire, she read the curious words etched into the stone silently.

A burnt jewel. A hell demons throne. Both twins meet a fight.

'What do we suggest we do now?' The warden quizzed as she wiped the remnants of the Revenant's discoloured blood from her hands. 'If the Raven is as powerful as is suggested, would simply resurrecting more of them not lead to more disappointment?'

'For the moment the Revenants are a suitable distraction.' The masked man mused as she unhooked the black mask from his face. 'Keeping the Raven's attention away from the Society and our true intentions, by the time the prophecy comes to pass, it will be too late.'

'He will know of our involvement. even he knows the Revenants must be directed in order to take form in this world.'

'Distractions, my dear. We provide him a world of distractions.'

'And if he finds the Ripper, what then?'

'You have a better suggestion?'

'Why don't we go loud with it all, use the system to detain him?'

'Go on.'

'In the spotlight, he will be forced to hide his powers. It will make hiding all the more difficult, and when they find him, we can act.'

'I feel this is a battle for the shadows.' The man mused as he wiped his face with the mask. 'But we shall let the coins decide.'

Reaching across the table, the man slid the warden's coin across to her and took his own. Admiring the engraved demon on the silver coin, he toyed with its weight in his hand before looking across at the warden.

'As the old ways were decided.' She declared, tossing the coin over in her hand. 'Our fates shall be decided by the coins.'

Both of them tossed their coin into the air and watched as they arced over onto the table. Both coins landed at the same time on the table and bounced around before settling one next to the other. The masked man's coin remained upturned with the two-horned demon looking up, while the warden's had landed face down with the blank side facing up.

'And so it is decided.' the man declared as he snatched back his coin. 'We shall keep this to the shadows.'

'So it shall be.'

Retrieving her own coin, the warden looked around the room and settled her attention on a display case to the side of the fireplace. Pocketing the silver coin, she walked across to the cabinet and admired the antique book that sat encased in the glass casing. The book sat open, its gilded leather cover secured in place and the pages separated by a weighty bookmark.

'Have you retrieved the pages?' She asked as she looked at the parchment pages.

'Not yet.' The masked man confessed as he remained at the table. 'We are in the process of interrogating the one who last had them.'

'Can we perform the ritual without them?'

'It will take longer, but it can still be done.'

'Good.'

Resting her hand on the glass casing, the warden was drawn to the intricate images and symbols etched onto the open pages of the leather book. The discoloured paper and pages looked strikingly similar to the pages John had recovered from the London apartment. Although the typography of the symbols was slightly different, there was no denying, the pages were from the same source.

As the warden moved away from the case, the Revenant's severed head disintegrated into ash while its headless corpse had been draped over the centre of the three coffins on the far side of the room. The dark blood that oozed from the wounds stained the pale stone and pooled on the floor below. Ignoring the grotesque display, the warden offered another respectful nod and made her way for the doors, leaving the once masked man alone in the eerie crypt.

'May the wings of dark angels protect you, Qamar.' The warden offered as she walked past him.

'And you too, Diana.'

Keeping his attention on the upturned coin on the table, Qamar waited for the door to close before he allowed himself to visibly relax. Letting out a long breath, he turned to rest on the edge of the table and stared at the bloodied corpse atop the ancient coffin.

17

— · —

A RIPPER'S ECHO

Whitechapel at night still had the same feel in John's mind. Perhaps it was the fact he was once again treading the same path towards the scene of a murder, but it was like the soul of the small borough remained the same while the exterior simply shrouded its true nature. Returning to the scene of the most recent murder, John's mind struggled to find balance. As he walked beside Kimberley, more than once his memories encroached on his vision and he found his view of the world oddly distorted between past and present.

'We really need to do something about the way you dress.' Kimberley remarked as they left the main road and passed through a narrow alleyway.

'There's nothing wrong with how I look.'

Wearing the long coat and curious, almost steampunk, style of clothing, it was certainly not a conspicuous outfit. Even though he wasn't wearing the plague doctor mask, Kimberley felt it would have done little to change the sideways glances from the people they passed.

'You're not really fitting in.'

'How should I look?' John snapped as he paused beneath a flickering streetlight and wiped his hands down his coat.

As his hand passed along the leather, the clothes beneath changed from a waistcoat and shirt to a tight-fitted high-neck top and combat trousers. Keeping the jet-black boots, John brushed himself down for effect and slowly turned to get Kimberley's approval.

'And the coat?'

'That stays!' John quickly replied, fiddling with the collar. 'It's part of who I am.'

'Really? It's hardly cold enough for a coat like that. You must be boiling.'

'Not really a problem, is it?' John chuckled. 'But the rest of it, does that meet your requirements?'

'It'll do.' Kimberley groaned as she moved past John, continuing along the alleyway. 'So, what's with the coat?'

'It was the only thing I kept with me.' John's voice dwindled a little. 'It was the one thing I went home and got, it means a lot to me.'

'It's seen better days.' Kimberley remarked as she admired the scuffs and roughly sewn-up cuts and damage.

'I could fix it, like I did changing my clothes, but I use it as a reminder.'

Trailing off, it was clear Kimberley had hit a nerve and dared not to push as they navigated the side streets. Once again moving in silence, John could feel her eyes on him every so often, but kept his attention fixed on where they were heading. Turning onto the street where John had broken into the crime scene, they once again saw the idling police van at the far end of the street.

'How do you want to play this?' Kimberley quizzed as John moved past and dropped to her knees, clutching his chest. 'Are you alright?'

Having entered the quiet street, John had caught sight of the police van, but something else had stolen his attention. Passing by Kimberley, he felt a sudden jolt of electricity course through his body. It was a feeling he had felt only once before, when the Ripper had ripped the life from his body. As he dropped to his knees, hands clutching at the place where the Ripper's wounds had been, the modern world around him collapsed and was replaced with a distorted vision of the merged worlds of past and present.

Desperate to break free of the glitching vision, John could hear Kimberley's voice, but she was not part of the world with him at that moment. Blinking, hoping to break free of the vision, John scanned his surroundings and settled his attention on an all too familiar silhouette at the far end of the street. All muscle, still dressed in the top-hat and tails of the Victorian era, John could see the Ripper watching him.

'Why are you here?' John Screamed but his voice was muted, no words escaping his lips. 'You were banished.'

'You really are not the sentinel this world needs.' The Ripper hissed as it moved towards him.

'What do you want from me?'

'You'll find out soon enough.' The Ripper declared and sprinted the remaining distance between them until it was on him.

Crashing to the tarmac, John closed his eyes and felt a wave of relief as Kimberley's panicked voice suddenly filled his senses. Opening his eyes, John was glad to see the world had returned to its normal view, modern London once again his surroundings with no sign of the Victorian distortions or the Ripper lingering in the shadows.

'What the hell was that about?'

'Nothing.' John fought to catch his breath as he scanned every dark corner and shadow for signs of the Ripper. 'It was nothing.'

'It didn't look like nothing.'

'Come on, we need to get moving. We're already drawing attention.' John changed the subject and motioned across at the curious police officer now sauntering towards them.

'That's on you.' Kimberley groaned as she moved to speak with the officer.

Still somewhat disorientated, John struggled to his feet and looked across at Kimberley. Deep in conversation with the officer, John took a moment to calm his racing mind.

'Puppets, all of them.' The Ripper's familiar voice oozed from the darkness as John snatched his attention back to the police officer.

Allowing his senses to tune to the world between life and death, John saw the tethers of darkness attached to the police officer. Knowing the man was not what he seemed, John pushed past Kimberley and landed a solid blow in the officer's throat.

'Are you crazy!?!' Kimberley shrieked as she jumped back.

John landed a second blow on the side of the man's head and in response, the unconscious officer slumped to the ground at his feet. Staring down at the officer, John rolled him over with his foot, and Kimberley saw her answer. The officer's face contorted despite being unconscious and Kimberley could only watch as a sickly black liquid oozed out of his eyes, nose and mouth onto the pavement.

'Step back.' John warned as the liquid pooled on the ground next to the police officer. 'That's not something you want on your pretty shoes, or anywhere else, for that matter.'

'What is it?'

'That's from the Ripper's touch.' John mused as he once again scanned their surroundings. 'He's not far, or at least he's been here recently.'

'Will he be alright, him that is?' Kimberley looked down at the unconscious officer.

'He'll have no memory of what happened.' John inspected the pool of ooze as it finished seeping from the officer's eyes. 'It hadn't been there long. There's just enough to assume control, nothing else.'

'What else could it have done to him?'

'It would have killed him. I call it the Leech. It allows the Ripper to control its victims until the point he can use their body for food. At that point, those victims will willingly present themselves for consumption.'

'That's disgusting.'

'Nothing about this is pretty, Kimberley.' John admired the liquid as it slowly evaporated, leaving a dark stain on the ground.

'Where's it gone?'

'Without a host, it has no life. It's nothing more than the essence of death and decay, like a virus.' John checked the unconscious officer's pulse. 'You never want that stuff inside you. It's pure evil.'

Moving away from the slumbering officer, John turned his attention towards the taped off murder scene. Sensing the closeness of the Ripper, John knew they needed to act fast. Although the street was empty, it wouldn't be long before curious eyes would see the police officer and they would no longer have the time they needed to make their enquiries in the scene.

'Help me with him.' John barked as he hoisted the officer from the tarmac.

'What are we going to do with him?'

'Put him back in there.' John motioned towards the idling police van. 'After that, we won't have long.'

Carrying the weight between them, they secured the officer back in the driver's seat without being disturbed by any passersby. Dropping his hat over his face, John closed the door and looked at Kimberley. Her face told a very different story than his own. He could see the concern on her face, and he knew he had pushed her beyond the limits of her comfort again.

'You don't look happy.' John scoffed as he ducked under the scene tape.

'How can I be?' Kimberley snapped as she followed behind. 'here I am, helping an escaped convict and breaking into a murder scene. It might all be in a day's work for you, but it's a new experience for me.'

'Exciting isn't it?'

'Not really, no!' Kimberley snapped as she grabbed his shoulder and turned him to face her. 'I don't know how much deeper I can go down this hole with you.'

'You're in too deep now. Even if you were to leave my side, you're already seen the lengths the warden has gone to by using the Revenants.'

Pulling away, John continued along into the dark alley with Kimberley hot on his heels.

'I still don't get how she's messed up with things like that. I mean, does she even know they exist?'

'That I'm not sure about, yet. If she's enlisted the assistance of the Society, I expect she either has connections and knows everything, or else she's foolishly now in their debt. Either way, it's something that's been bugging me.'

'I could ask her.'

'You'd go back to the Nuthall, knock on the door and just ask the old warden?'

'I could.'

'And I expect they'd kill you.'

'She's not like that.' Kimberley protested as they reached the murder scene. 'She may be many things, but she isn't a killer.'

'That's not a chance I'll let you take. I have a responsibility to keep you safe. After all, it's my fault you're in this mess.'

John's mood took a sombre turn and, for the first time, he showed an essence of an emotion that Kimberley had not seen since they had first met in the interview room. Not wanting to wallow in the moment, John turned his attention to the array of evidence markers spread around the alley. Numbered markers remained in the same position since when he had last visited, but now a forensic tent had been erected in the centre of the alley.

'This wasn't here last time.'

Moving to the tent, John pulled aside the door of the tent and jumped back in response. Catching Kimberley by surprise, John launched back and pushed her behind him, shielding him from whatever had startled him.

'What's going on?' Kimberley pressed as she pushed to look past his hulking frame.

'He's been here.' John hissed. 'Recently. Very recently.'

Pushing through his arm, Kimberley stopped dead in her tracks at what she saw. Unsure of what she expected, the sight that greeted her was nothing like what she had thought. Inside the centre of the tent, the shadowy outline of a demonic figure hung in the air above the floor. Kimberley knew it was not a person, but the shadowy echo of the Ripper. Even though the tendrils of smoke moved in the air, she could make out enough of the detail to see the figure of a man crouched above the ground.

'What is that?'

'It's an echo of the Ripper.' John inched closer. 'Take my hand. This won't be pleasant.'

'What won't be?'

'There isn't the time to explain.'

Taking her hand, John moved towards the fading silhouette of smoke and pressed his hand towards it. As he did so, the plague doctor mask materialised on his face once again and all Kimberley could do was clamp her eyes shut and grab hold of John's arm. The moment his fingers touched the floating tendrils of smoke, both of them were ripped from where they stood.

Dragged into the smouldering silhouette, Kimberley felt her stomach lurch as if someone had dropped her off a cliff. Her skin felt alive with pain, like a thousand hot needles pressing against her. As she struggled to find breath, she opened her eyes and saw nothing but the plague doctor mask and a swirling world of jet-black smoke around her.

After what felt like an age, Kimberley felt the ground beneath her feet and, once again, the air rushed into her lungs. Collapsing to the ground, she clutched at her chest and looked up to see John once again as the Raven standing beside her as if nothing had happened. Turning to look down at her, she heard his muffled voice from within the mask.

'No matter what happens, stay away from him.'

John's attention was fixed on the Ripper, who stood proud above the corpse of a young woman.

18

— • —

MITRE SQUARE

E ven cloaked in its modern visage, John knew where he was, and how the Ripper had come to be here. Although out of sequence, and not within Whitechapel, John was all-too-familiar with Mitre Square and the murder of Catherine Eddowes. On the night of her murder, John had sought out the Ripper, much as he had this night, and disturbed it mid-attack. Having arrived in time to see it bleed the life from Elizabeth Stride, John had done all he could but despite everything the woman had died. In his obsession with saving Catherine, he had given the Ripper time to commit its next murder.

'You should run.' John hushed from behind the mask and looked across at the Ripper.

Once again the world took on its split appearance as his memories fought to cast their shadow over his view of the present moment. Glitching visions of the past obscured his full view of the world, but John ignored it and kept his attention on the Ripper, and the mutilated corpse at its feet.

'I've been expecting you. Sooner than this.' The Ripper's voice croaked as it lifted a bloodstained hand from the corpse's torso.

'Well, here I am.' John pulled the escrima sticks from his back and clenched them in his trembling hands.

'You'll need those.'

'I'm better trained than when we last met, and look what happened back then.'

'Oh, you don't need them for me.' The Ripper chuckled, it's menacing laugh echoing bouncing off the curious mix of old and new architecture. 'You'll need it for them.'

Pointing its bloodstained hand skyward, John raised his attention and saw the faces of a dozen smaller creatures attached to the front a large high-rise office block overlooking the square. Recognising them immediately, John split his attention between the gathered creatures and the Ripper.

'Giving up already?' John scoffed, the feigned confidence betrayed by the nervousness in his voice.

'I have things to attend to.' The Ripper declared as it lowered itself back down and returned its attention to the mutilated corpse.

Before John could protest at the Ripper's grotesque dismemberment of the dead woman's body, the winged creatures on the building attacked. Small in stature, they resembled winged demons from artwork, but John knew exactly what they were. Imps, as these were, offered themselves as simple warriors and soldiers. Driven only by their desire to fight, their diminutive size gave them an advantage in combat, coupled with their wings.

The first dove-bombed down towards John and he had no choice but to tear his attention from the Ripper and concentrate on holding back the onslaught of aerial attacks from the Imps. Making sure he kept the flaying creature's attention on him, John hoped Kimberley would take advantage of the distraction and make her escape from the square. Knowing she was so close to the Ripper, and he was distracted by the Imps, he dreaded what could happen.

Grabbing the nearest of the Imps, John set about ripping the wings from its back and sending it crashing into the side of a parked car. As the Imp collided with the door of the car, it exploded in a shower of stone and dust as it turned into a stone statue. With the dented chassis and smashed window left in its wake, the only thing that remained of the Imp was the crumbled head of stone on the floor.

'Help me!' Kimberley shrieked as one Imp took hold of her back and tried to lift her into the air.

Casting aside the sneaky attack from another of the flying demons, John rolled across the tarmac on his shoulder to avoid the collision and launched up into the air. Slamming the escrima stick at the flying Imp's head, he felt the resistance and swelled with pride as the Imp's head exploded in a cloud of dust and debris. Grateful the creature hadn't lifted Kimberley too high from the ground, she landed at the same time he did.

Taking hold of her sleeve, John dragged Kimberley up and over the damaged car as the relentless onslaught continued from the other Imps.

'You need to get away from here.' John snapped as he deflected another attack.

'Where am I going to go?'

'As far from me as possible.'

'That's not exactly helpful!' Kimberley bit as John caught an Imp mid-flight and slammed its wings through the glass of the passenger door. 'I can't go back to my normal life now, can I?'

Taking hold of both wings, John set about pulling them apart until they snapped away from the Imp's back. Shrieking with pain, the wingless demon dropped to the floor and ducked beneath the car as the wings in John's hands disintegrated. Brushing his hands, John retrieved the escrima sticks from the floor and offered out a hand for Kimberley.

'You can hide here.'

'What?' She quizzed as she took his ungloved hand.

As their skin touched, Kimberley knew what he had done. Mid-protest, she once again felt herself dragged into the world of John's memories and the world around her collapsed. Shielding herself from the crumbling walls and buildings, Kimberley watched as Victorian London once again built itself around her in terrifying detail.

'Find the clues from this murder in my memories, and I will deal with the present.' John's voice echoed from the heavy dark clouds that lumbered overhead.

'I don't know where to start.' Kimberley protested but fell silent as she drank in her surroundings.

Kimberley found herself still in Mitre Square, but the scene was very different. Where the tall office buildings had been standing were now the typical Victorian houses and structures, you would expect to find in London. There was already a hive of activity as the distant chimes of Big Ben tolled in the air.

'Two in the morning and that bastard has struck again.' A cockney voice declared from behind her. 'Coppers say she's still warm.'

Following the gaze of the two men held in hushed conversation, Kimberley caught sight of a pale-faced constable standing in front of a bloodstained sheet draped on the ground. Already knowing what was to come, Kimberley realised the body was in the opposite corner from where she had seen the Ripper moments ago in the present. Pressing through the gathering crowds, Kimberley was careful not to interfere with any of the gathered people and made her way to the front.

'No further missy!' A stern officer barked as she approached and for a moment, Kimberley thought she had been seen.

'I need to know if it's Kate.'

'Listen here. There's nobody going to be seeing her tonight. You can come to the station in the morning and help us from there.'

'But...' The constable silenced the woman as he jabbed her roughly in the stomach with his truncheon.

'Bastard.' The woman coughed as she backed away from the officer.

'You'll thank me when you see what he'd done to the poor lass.'

Moving beyond the constable, Kimberley scanned the crowd as the woman made her way back across Mitre Square. Losing her amongst the sea of faces, Kimberley turned her attention back to the crime scene and stopped dead in her tracks as she almost collided with Inspector Abberline. As ever, the Inspector was dressed immaculately, and took a moment to scan the surroundings before moving to the shrouded corpse. Motioning to the pale-faced young officer, the Inspector moved to the body as the sheet was lifted aside.

Careful to keep the disturbing view from the crowds and the eyes of the journalists that had already gathered, Kimberley had to move herself alongside Abberline to get a view. Kimberley felt her stomach churn as the sickening sight beneath the sheet came into view. Closing her eyes, she longed to forget the image of the dismembered and bloodied corpse on the cobblestones.

'I've seen enough.' Abberline croaked as he held a handkerchief to his mouth. 'It's getting too familiar seeing this monster's handiwork.'

'What do you want us to do?' The pale officer asked as he replaced the sheeting and stepped back.

'I'll have you relieved from the scene and you can return with me to the station for a statement.' Abberline scribbled notes in a small pad as he spoke. 'The pathologist will be here soon and I expect they will remove the body before sunrise.'

'There's something else, Inspector.' The nervousness in the constable's voice piqued both Abberline and Kimberley's attention.

'Go on.'

'There were markings, near the body.' The young man looked unnerved. 'That's what caught my attention first.'

'Did they look like this?' Abberline thumbed through the pages and thrust the page towards the constable.

'Yes, sir.'

'Show me.'

Calling for another officer to replace him by the shrouded body, the constable led Abberline behind a small wall and into a narrow alleyway a little way away from the body. Immediately, Kimberley could see the inscriptions, once again painted in blood.

'You saw these first?' Abberline pressed as she scribbled a crude version of the images in his notebook.

'Yes, sir. I walked along from there, you see, and when I found this, I knew something wasn't right.'

'How so?'

'I probably shouldn't say.'

'Tonight is not the night for tight lips.' Abberline snapped as he finished his sketch. 'Speak plainly, boy, or else your next posting will make this look like a walk in the park.'

'I heard about similar things being seen at murders before. Strange words scribble on the walls in blood.'

Abberline rounded on the constable in a heartbeat and grabbed the young man by the collar. Pressing him back against the wall, Abberline moved his face close to the younger man's so only he could hear him.

'Who told you about that?'

'I'd rather not...' Abberline silenced his with a sharp back-hand across the face.

'Don't test me, constable.'

'John Smith, he told me about them before they killed him.'

'He did, did he?' Abberline mused as he glared at the younger man. 'What else did that loose-lipped fool tell you?'

'Only that they'd found markings like this at all of Jack's murders.'

'You say *they* killed him? Who do you think that would be?'

'Whoever is helping Jack get away with this. It's nigh on impossible to do this and not be seen. He's got to be getting help, and powerful help at that.'

'Keep thoughts like that to yourself.' Abberline warned as he released his grip on the officer and brushed down his uniform. 'Meet me at the station by three, I'll make sure your position is relieved.'

'Yes, sir.'

'And speak nothing of this.' Abberline wafted his hand towards the array of symbols and curious letters.

Not giving the constable any chance to answer, Abberline smoothed out his coat and stalked back out of the alley, leaving him alone in the dark shadows. Seeing the young man shaking, Kimberley realised how on edge the whole of London was. Little did the memories of John's past know of the significance of these murders for years yet to come. Even before Kimberley had found herself embroiled in the darker truths of the murder, there wasn't a living soul who had not heard of Jack The Ripper and his heinous crimes. Only now, as Kimberley explored the even darker truth about the Ripper, did she realise what dangers and evils lurked in the shadows.

Casting aside the sudden surge of fear that washed over her, she pressed past the constable and made her way along the alley.

'You shouldn't be here, all alone, as you are.' The voice declared from a shadowed doorway to her side.

'You can see me?' Kimberley gasped as she quickly put space between her and the dark recess.

'Of course I can, Kimberley.' Hearing her name sent an icy chill down her spine as a figure emerged from the doorway. 'You have nothing to fear, I'm not here to hurt you.'

Unsure of how to feel, Kimberley was relieved it wasn't the Ripper that had announced her name from the shadows. As the visage of Death stepped out of the shadows, she felt a wave of confusion at feeling relief.

'How can you see me?'

'Because I'm more than just a passive memory.' Death explained as he once again removed the heavy hood from his head and Kimberley watched the human face grown around the exposed skull. 'I'm surprised my Raven would allow you the freedom to stalk his memories unguided.'

'He was busy.'

'Curious answer.' Death mused as he stepped closer to her. 'Shall we return to the crime and see if I can't point you in the right direction?'

'Isn't this causing ripples? Me talking to you that is?'

'Ripples?' Death chuckled as he looked at Kimberley. 'You know more than I would have expected.'

'Clearly not enough.'

'Touche!'

19

ESCAPE

With Kimberley lost in his memories, John was torn between the past and present, even more so than he had been. Doing his best to blank out Kimberley's echoing footsteps in the recesses of his mind, he concentrated on fighting back against the constant onslaught of Imps that rained down on him. With Kimberley's corpse frozen in situ beside the now battered car, he knew she remained invisible to the conscious world, as she was now shrouded in the same dark magic that kept him from the attention of the living.

Hoping that the shroud would be enough to keep the Imps, and more importantly the Ripper's, attention from her, John continued to fight for survival.

'You seem tired.' The Ripper taunted as it lifted the severed heart from the dead woman's chest. 'Hardly the sentinel of these pitiful people, hardly the Raven anymore.'

Enraged by the Ripper's taunts, John pressed his weight against the side of the car and kicked it across the tarmac towards the demon. As the car lurched forward, John felt a solid blow against the side of his head as an Imp crashed a heavy stone fist into him. Knocked off-balance by the sudden attack, John fought to keep his balance and used his enhanced senses to predict the trajectory of the incoming attacks.

Sensing the movement, John ducked aside but found himself overpowered by a trio of winged creatures that crashed into him. Feeling his arms dragged down by his sides, the creatures restricted his movements and they fought to pin him back against the wall on the far side of the square. Fighting against the tight grip of the Imps, John felt his head pummelled from either side as blow after blow was rained down on him.

Fighting to keep his mind calm enough to hold Kimberley safe in his memories, John collected his senses and launched up into the air. Once again, John moved with impossible speed, but so too did the Imps that clung to his torso. Climbing high above Mitre Square, John dislodged two of the Imps and cleanly snapped the wings from their backs and watched them crash to the floor below.

Seeing surrounding London in a state of slow motion, John took a moment to calm his mind as he caught movement out of his peripheral vision. Waiting until the last moment, John met the Imp's attack with a precisely aimed fist that ripped through the creature's chest. Once again, the demonic creature disintegrated to dust and stone around his arm as John looked down for any sign of the Ripper.

Seeing only the mutilated corpse, John scanned the square but saw no sign of the Ripper anywhere. Suspended in mid-air, he rose higher still until he could see the streets beyond in all directions.

'Where have you gone, you sneaky bastard?' John hushed into the mask as he scanned his surroundings for any echo of the Ripper's movements.

Seeing an essence of darkness in the distance, John could not chance leaving Kimberley alone in the now empty square. Cursing his circumstances, John looked down as two of the Imps directed her attention to the frozen woman below. Dropping back down to the ground, John intercepted the two Imps and once again made quick work of despatching the pair of them. As a third attacked, John caught the creature mid-flight and pulled its twisted face close to the plague doctor mask.

'Where's your master going?' John growled as he landed back on the ground and held the Imp in front of him.

'Maybe you should care more about your toy than the Ripper.' John followed the Imp's gaze down towards Kimberley, who was now convulsing on the ground.

'What have you done to her?'

'Nothing. It's all you, all up there.' The Imp tapped its finger against John's hood and in response he crushed the Imp's neck.

Dropping to the ground, John scooped his arms beneath Kimberley and wrapped them both beneath the heavy leather coat. Knowing he would be vulnerable, John pressed his hand against Kimberley's face and followed her into his memories.

Immediately, John found himself back in the familiar surroundings of Victorian London. Drinking in the rich tapestry of London life, he scanned the nighttime streets for any sign of Kimberley. Over the sea of curious bystanders, John looked towards the two constables engrossed in conversation next to the covered corpse but saw no sign of Kimberley.

'Kimberley?' John hissed as he ripped the plague doctor's mask from his face. 'Where are you?'

Feeling the eyes of the nearest people turn towards him, he knew he was pushing too much against the confines of his own memories. Conscious of the ripples he would be causing, John pushed through the crowd and felt their hands groping at his coat. Reaching the front of the crowd, John pushed towards the covered body and found his path blocked by the muscular constable.

'You're going nowhere mate.' The constable growled as he grabbed John's arm. 'This ain't no place for onlookers. Now get back.'

Knowing the ripples were swelling, John stepped back and offered his apologies. Pulling free from his grip, John cursed as he moved back through the crowds. Thrashing out, John's mind raced as he tried to centre himself on the moment of this memory. He knew the body in Mitre Square belonged to Catherine Eddowes, the second victim of that particular night, and he also knew this was not the Ripper's next murder after the one at Durward Street.

'What's going on?' John barked as he kicked out at a pile of debris by the side of the street.

As soon as the debris scattered around the street, the entire crowd turned to face him. A sea of eyes glared at John as he stood on the cobbled street.

'Oh, shit.'

The crowd surged forward and John knew he had gone too far. Drawing the attention of the figures in his memories, John turned and ran. Even without looking back, he could hear the slap of feet as he raced through the labyrinthine alleyways away from Mitre Square. Sensing the world closing around, John knew he had to move fast to find Kimberley and get them out.

Sprinting past the St Botolph church, John launched over the railings and dived behind the rear of the church. Taking refuge behind an ivy-covered gravestone, John watched as the confused faces scanned around for their prey. Waiting for the crowds to disappear, John emerged from the graveyard and moved through the side streets, doing his best to remain unseen.

Unlike his presence in the outside world, his ability to remain invisible was not as simple as distracting attention from unconscious minds. In his own memories, John knew his senses were alert and searching for infiltrators, even if it was himself exploring his own memories.

Feeling for Kimberley's presence, he could feel nothing. Frustrated by her absence, John pushed through the streets and came to a stop at a narrow t-junction. Looking both ways, a sudden scream snatched his attention, and he moved in a heartbeat. Focussing his attention on the echoes of the terrified scream, John found himself in familiar territory as he surged along Goulston Street.

'Kimberley?' He hissed as he skidded to a halt.

Kimberley was laid on the floor, convulsing as she had been on the tarmac of Mitre Square. In an instant, John cursed himself for being so ignorant. Grateful for the darkness of the heavy shadows and night, John bent down and took Kimberley in his arms.

'What happened to you?' John hushed as he brushed the hair from her face.

Turning his attention to the shadowy archway, John read the text scrawled across the wooden door.

The Juwes are the men that will not be blamed for nothing.

Knowing this was the only message linked to Jack the Ripper, John felt his heart sink as he saw the chalk stains on Kimberley's fingers. This was nothing new. He had seen the shaking letters thousands of times over the years. He even remembered first seeing it in very similar circumstances. Confused by the circle of consequences, John knew it was time to take Kimberley back.

'What's going on?' John hissed as he closed his eyes and withdrew them from the dark memory.

Returning to Mitre Square, John shielded Kimberley's face from the bright sunlight as her body relaxed and his coat slipped free.

'Where am I?' Her voice croaked.

'You're back. Take a moment.'

John looked around the square and realised they were alone. The Imps no longer launched themselves from every building and they found themselves surrounded by an eerie and awkward silence.

'Where is the Ripper?'

'I don't know.' John confessed as he helped her to sit back against the battered car. 'I lost him when I came after you.'

'What about her?' Kimberley raised a trembling hand and pointed to the bloodied corpse on the far side of the square.

Knowing what he would see, John knew he needed to see the destruction the Ripper had left behind. Making sure Kimberley was alright, John brushed himself down and moved across to the motionless corpse. Blood stained the pavement beneath the body and even John, having seen all he had over the years, felt revulsion at the woman's body.

'She's gone.' John offered, his voice devoid of any emotion.

Scanning the jagged wounds, John realised how far the Ripper had gone this time. The woman's heart lay discarded beside her open and hand and all John could do to offer her respect was to drape his coat over her body. Ensuring there was nothing left on show for any passerby to find, John rose off his haunches and turned back to look at Kimberley.

'Freeze.' A voice boomed from across the square and John rounded in an instant.

Having draped the coat over the dead woman's body, he had revealed himself for all to see. Transitioning into view of the living world completely, he had exposed himself to the pair of armed police officers that now levelled their weapons at him.

'Listen,' John began but his voice was drowned out by the almost panicked instructions barked by the pair of officers.

'Stay where you are, drop to your knees. Keep your hands on show.'

A second police car screamed past the first that sat short at the junction into Mitre Square and John found himself bathed int he red and blue strobes. Two more armed officers launched from the car and quickly flanked him to block off any chance of escape. Knowing he was trapped, John caught Kimberley's gaze and felt relief as she shuffled around the back of the battered car and struggled to her feet.

'Drop down.' One of the other officers barked as John saw the red and green lasers dancing over his torso and legs. 'Get on your god damned knees.'

'I'm not going to offer you any resistance.'

'Then do as you're told. NOW!'

Stalling enough to give Kimberley time to stagger across to the alleyway out of the square, John laboured his compliance enough to keep the nervous officers' attention on him.

'What's under there?'

'You don't want to look.'

'Listen pal, we'll decide what's goin on. Hands on your head.'

Interlocking his fingers on top of his head, John weighed up his options. Although he could have escaped the officers, this was not the time, or place. Exposed as he was to the living world, it would risk too much to use his powers to escape. Knowing the safer option was to play along, he waited patiently for the approaching officer to set the handcuffs against his wrist and fasten them in position.

'Secure.' The officer boomed as he locked both John's arms behind his back. 'Now, what's underneath the coat.'

'You're obviously here for a reason.' John hushed. 'You must have an idea.'

Twisting John's head around, the second officer gripped the leather coat and pulled it back.

'I wouldn't if I were you.' But it was too late.

Once again the mutilated body was exposed for the world to see. Feeling revulsion at the disregard the Ripper had paid to his unfortunate victim, John tried to turn his attention away but felt the tight grip of the police officer forcing him to look.

'You're under arrest for murder.'

'Wrong guy.' John flippantly replied as the officer recited the caution.

In a matter of minutes John was thrust hard against the side of the nearest police vehicle and found himself thrown into the back seat, coming to rest against a large metal box that sat across most of the back seat. Adjusting his awkward position enough, John watched the four officers gather at the front of the police vehicle. One of them looked pale and clammy, the sight of the mutilated corpse had clearly had an effect on the young man and he simply watched through the misty glass as the four men tried to make sense of what they had found.

Knowing his time was limited, John took advantage of the distraction and allowed himself to call upon his dark gift and disappeared from the back seat of the police car.

'Listen you psychotic bastard..' One of the officers growled as the rear door was pulled open.

The sentence was never finished as the officer stood staring at the now empty seat of the police vehicle. Allt hat remained of John was the pair of handcuffs that now sat on the leather seat. Dumbfounded the young officer snatched up the cuffs and inspected the fact they were still locked and secure. Turning around the young man scanned the square for any signs of movement, any signs of his escaped prisoner.

There was nothing moving as the officer looked, only the leather coat that fluttered in the gentle breeze and a raven that sat on the far wall watching them.

EPISODE

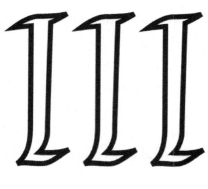

THE RIPPER

20

DEATH MESSAGE

J ohn sat on the edge of Tower Bridge with the traffic flowing beneath him. Unseen by the world, he was bathed in the pale moonlight as he held the folded parchment sheet in the light of the spotlight at his side.

'What has any of this got to do with where I'm going?' John mused as he admired the curious text and symbols that covered the page.

Having stared at the sheet he had recovered from the nameless man for the last three nights, John was still at a loss for where it all fit in. Having escaped Mitre Square, leaving the confused officers staring into the back of the empty police car, he had struggled to find any sign of Kimberley. At first, his fears had naturally fallen to the idea the Ripper had found her, but now he was certain he had not.

Since the grisly murder in Mitre Square, the media had pounced on the fact the most recent series of murders were paying homage to Jack The Ripper's urban legend. While the general population believed it to be nothing more than a copycat killer, John knew otherwise. Knowing the Ripper was still out there, he folded the paper and returned his attention to the London skyline. With the flashing beacon of Canary Wharf behind him, John's attention fell naturally to the impressively illuminated Tower of London.

Since his death, London had changed. John had watched the new world grow around him until he had surrendered himself to the Nuthall Hospital. Back then it had been under a different name, and the wing he had occupied when he had first met Kimberley had been all around the building. Over the decades of his imprisonment, John had watched the building change, much as he knew the world would have outside.

Grateful to see familiar remnants of the past he remembered, he found the current view of London a disturbing reflection of his memories. The twisted distortions between past and present were almost mirrored in the landscape of the capital. For every dozen modern buildings, all angular and glass-fronted, there remained the relics of London's rich history. It was seeing these that gave John at least a semblance of connection to w world he no longer belonged in.

In the nights that had passed since his arrest at Mitre Square, he had moved no closer to the Ripper. There had been the expected media frenzy, but the Ripper himself had gone quiet. Even as he scoured the usual haunts of the demon, he saw no tell-tale whispers or echoes the creature had even been there. Frustrated beyond measure, John had even returned to Kimberley's apartment and found no sign she had been back. Desperate to find any sign of either of them, John cleared his mind and searched the city from his vantage point for anything he could follow.

'You're not going to find her here.' Death's familiar voice taunted.

John jumped to his feet and balanced on the perilous ledge above the flowing traffic. Searching all around, he saw no sign of Death among the shadows created by the bright spotlights.

'You pick a funny time to speak to me.' John snapped as he saw no sign of Death. 'You've left me alone long enough, I thought you'd given up.'

'Not as much as you gave up on yourself.' Death scorned as the visage of death melted out of a heavy shadow across from John. 'Hiding in the confines of that prison was not what I expected from my Raven.'

'I had nothing left to do.' John boomed as he jumped onto a higher beam to move closer to Death. 'I honoured my oath in facing the Ripper. It may have taken me longer than you would have liked, but I honoured it.'

'Did you?' Death mocked as he moved along the narrow beam. 'If that were true, you wouldn't still be here.'

John knew Death's meaning. His oath had been one of service and protection. While John had believed he had banished the Ripper, all signs now pointed to a failed duty. The concept was not lost on him, and John was haunted by the decisions he had made in recent years. Not that he would ever admit as much to Azrael.

'Clearly I was wrong!' John offered with a flamboyant bow of his torso. 'I offer my humblest of apologies, oh seer of all.'

'Sarcasm really is your default, isn't it?'

Death ripped back the heavy hood that shrouded his face and John watched as the skin reformed around the exposed human skull. Once the familiar face of Azrael had settled in place, John dared to speak. Having seen the curious rebirth of a face on bone, almost a reverse death, John still could not shake the eerie feeling when he saw it happen with his own eyes.

'You've aged, getting ready for retirement?'

'Closer than you'd know.' Azrael confessed as he lowered to sit opposite John. 'The afterlife is a dark and dangerous place of late, more so than it has ever been.'

'And I suppose that's my fault?'

'Not everything is about you.' Azrael scoffed as John sat on the far side of the wide opening between the support pillars of the bridge. 'But my having to come here is a distraction I do not need right now.'

'I didn't ask you to come.'

'Really? How many hours have you spent talking to the shadows, hoping I would offer you guidance and answers?'

The feigned smirk of confidence disappeared from John's face as he recalled the many times he had hoped to find answers in the shadows, just as Azrael had proclaimed. Awash with frustration and embarrassment, John steered the conversation in a new direction.

'Have you watched from the sidelines, or are you ignorant of what's been happening while you've been busy?' Fighting to keep his voice level, John waited for an answer.

'I've kept my ear to the ground and half an eye on you.' Azrael hushed from across the gap. 'It's not my place to steer you. It was always your job to hold your perch and watch.'

'My duty was done.' John bit back. 'I banished the Ripper into the catacombs.'

'Evidently not.'

The simple reply was scathing, and John fought back the surge of frustration that rushed through him. Glaring across at Azrael, he knew the best way to react was simply to accept the almost teacher-like scorning he knew was coming. Taking a moment, John composed himself enough to sound calmer than he felt.

'How is it he's back then? I found the tombs and completed the ritual, as I understood it to be.'

'That is not your greatest concern right now.' Azrael replied as he watched the line of traffic ground to a halt below as an enormous ship approached along the Thames.

'Kimberley?'

'Yes. The innocent you dragged into our world. You have a duty to protect her. It was your decision to bring her here, and now she stands vulnerable to a world she should not have seen.'

'I had no choice. I needed someone to help me break free.'

'Only because you surrendered yourself there.' It was Azrael's turn to raise his voice as he rose to stand on the narrow beam. 'You gave them everything to contain and curtail you.'

'I had no direction. I was left to be nothing.'

'You were their protector. Just because your fight was done doesn't mean your duty was.' Azrael snapped as he replaced the hood over his head. 'Of all people, I would have thought you would have understood that.'

'Understand what? You told me nothing.'

'Maybe I was wrong in choosing you.' Azrael mused as he made his way across the beams to join John. 'Maybe I should have let the Ripper have its way with you that night in Whitechapel?'

'Piss off!'

Azrael moved like lightning. Taking hold of John's collar, he pushed him off balance and held him at an awkward angle above the cars below. As the sails of the ship moved through the raised bridge, John glared into the empty shadow of Azrael's hood. Knowing the lifeless eyes were watching him from within, he did his best to hold his resolve and refused to hold on to Azrael's skinless hand that held onto him. Hearing the bridge closing beneath him, John waited for Azrael to speak.

'That young woman's fate is tied to yours now. Bring her back and we will see whether you are suitable to wear the honour of my Raven.' Staring into the shadow of Death's hood, John felt his unseen gaze. 'I charged you with protecting the living, not delivering them to evil. You owe me her soul, you owe her your protection.

Not giving him a chance to react or respond, Azrael released his grip on John's clothes and allowed him to fall to the ground below. Ensuring he was shrouded in the shadows to remain unseen, John called the plague doctor mask to his face and landed in the middle of the road as traffic once again flowed. As the cars and buses moved at a snail's pace around him, John looked up to where Azrael had been standing, but saw no sign of the hooded visage of Death. Ignoring the cars, John stalked along the white lines in the centre of the road and made his way back towards the impressive illuminated Tower of London.

As he moved between the flow of traffic, John dropped through the old gates onto the walkway alongside the old tower. Ignored by the handful of people, John looked towards the turbulent water of the Thames and stopped dead in his tracks. Hovering above the water were the all-too-familiar words he had seen scribbled on the wooden door in Goulston Street. The words now were not scribbled in chalk but shimmered as burning letters in the air, just above the surface of the water. He read them aloud again and felt his heart sink:

The Juwes are the men that will not be blamed for nothing.

Turning his attention back to the bridge, John caught sight of a solitary figure standing in the beam of light from the spotlight. Knowing the conjured words were the work of Azrael, John once again repeated them as the figure faded from view.

Knowing their meaning, John checked his surroundings and moved with the speed his powers allowed and navigated the London streets until he once again found himself standing in the familiar surroundings of Goulston Street.

It resembled nothing of what John remembered and as he looked at the vibrant array of restaurants and shopfronts; he longed for the familiar return of the facades from his memories. Despite the unfamiliar setting, John still knew where to stand and where the infamous words had once been scrawled on the wooden door. Looking around, John calmed his mind enough and watched as the world around him crumbled to dust and rebuilt itself from the foundations of his memories.

Where gaudy shopfronts had adorned the front of the old flat complex, the more familiar façade appeared before him. Knowing he was once again in the sanctuary of his mind, John allowed the world and its inhabitants to take their place around him and stepped aside as a horse and carriage trotted along the cobbled street towards him. While his location was as he remembered, there was a different feeling in the air. Scanning the sea of anonymous faces that went about their daily business, John finally settled his attention on the doorway where the letters had been written.

This was not the night of the murder. He could see no blood-stained apron of the Ripper's victim discarded on the stone step, nor could he see the letters scrawled in chalk on the door. In fact, for the first time, he realised there was no door in the recessed entry. Moving closer, he realised the door sat open with no view of what lay beyond the threshold.

'John?' An unfamiliar voice whispered from the shadows.

Knowing what he must do, John ignored the flow of people and moved towards the open door.

21

— · —

WHISPERING VOICES

The chatter of teeth echoed along the dimly lit hallway. Bathed in the flickering candlelight, John could feel the eyes drinking him in as he stalked along the hallway.

'You're not welcome here, Raven of Death.' An unfamiliar voice chattered through the walls. 'Turn back, leave these memories to us.'

Ignoring the taunts, John passed the rows of doors until he reached the base of a winding staircase. Looking up the centre of the staircase, John felt a wave of worry as the walls above were alive and moving. Taking a moment to allow his eyes to adjust, John realised the creatures that moved were Imps, perched atop the bannisters leading all the way to the upper levels of the dingy building.

'They slumber.' The voice oozed from the walls. 'But they smell your fear.'

'I'm here for the woman.'

'Which one?' We have many.'

Faces washed over John from every direction. Swimming around, he could make out no details as the faces swam in, around, and over him for a moment before they all disappeared.

'What are you?'

'You.' The voice chuckled from somewhere above. 'Maybe we should talk.'

The lights on the wall burst into life, illuminating his path to the upper levels of the building. Silently accepting the flickering invitation, John stalked up the stairs, every wary of the slumbering Imps that twitched as he moved past but kept their eyes closed. Keeping one hand on the escrima stick at his back, John moved up the levels of the building, far more than he knew the building contained.

Whatever this place represented was something other than the building, as it had been. Knowing it had some deeper meaning, some representation of the depth and levels of his memory, John moved with caution until he reached the final landing.

To his surprise, he stood in front of the same door he remembered that marked the entrance to the building. The chalk letters once again adorned the pitted wooden door, and for a moment, John froze in position. Knowing the hibernating Imps surrounded him, he could feel their eyes on him but refused to pay them any attention. Still gripping the escrima stick in his left hand, John steadied his racing mind and reached for the handle on the door.

As his fingers touched the cold metal, the air was filled with the sound of breathing. The rhythmic inhale and exhale seemed almost too regulated and almost artificial as he unlocked the door and pushed it open.

'Welcome home.' The voice declared and John allowed his eyes to adjust to the darkness beyond the door.

At first, there was nothing beyond the door, only the amplified sound of breathing. Peering into the dark shadows, John gasped and lurched back as a figure came into view and took a handful of steps towards him until the figure paused at the threshold. Dumbstruck by what he saw, John saw a version of himself reflected in the open doorway. There were subtle differences in the masked Raven that stood facing him. The plague doctor mask looked somehow more weathered, and the figure's posture was not as tall as his own.

'Who are you?' John quizzed as he reached out to touch the curious apparition.

Reflecting his movements, the figure raised its own mirrored hand towards John. Rocking from side-to-side, John tested the limits of the strange figure which copied his every movement exactly. It was like looking in a mirror and as John inched closer, his reflection remain steadfast, framed by the door and unmoving.

'We are the same.' The voice hissed from behind the mask. 'Together on a path beyond life.'

For a moment, John couldn't figure if the voice was his own or something different. There were distinct familiarities, but something that wasn't quite him wasn't quite The Raven.

'Stop playing games.' John snapped as he reached to snatch the mask from the apparition's face.

Much to his surprise, John's hand passed through the figure in the doorway as if passing through smoke. Reforming in the wake of his movement, John struggled to make sense of what was happening and longed to bury his fist in the other Raven's face. Ripping the escrima stick from his back, John levelled the weapon at the other and saw the figure had not copied the movement. Standing unarmed, the other figure reached its hand to the mask on its face and slowly unclipped the leather straps at the back of its head. Keeping his weapon between them, John watched as the plague mask slipped free and, inch by inch, his own face appeared in front of him.

For the few seconds he saw his own reflection, John sensed a sudden change and lurched back as the figure in front of him morphed into the Ripper in a heartbeat. Discarding the mask, John readied himself as the muscular frame of the Ripper grew from his own reflection to fill the open door. Where there had been subtle differences in the Ripper in Mitre Square, this memory was *exactly* as he remembered the Ripper. Every inch of charred flesh, every pulsing vein and bulging muscle was as he had seen in his nightmares since the moment of his death.

'Where is she?' John spat as he glared at the Ripper.

'Providing me with everything I need.'

The Ripped burst from the threshold and John readied for the attack. Driving his weapon up through the air, he felt no impact as the wooden stick sliced up through the air and did nothing more than pass through the Ripper's body. Instantly, the figure exploded in a cloud of dust, forcing John to shield his face. As the cloud of dust passed over him, John returned his attention to the vacant doorway and could finally see what lay beyond. At odds with the decaying gothic interior of the old dosshouse, John now looked into a modern and sterile hospital room. Seeing London framed through the windows, bathed in sunshine, John wasn't sure where it was in terms of timeline.

Seeing only a pair of feet at the end of the bed, John moved through the door with caution and jumped as the chalked door slammed shut behind him. Enveloped in the sterile nature of the room, John once again heard the rhythmic artificial breaths from the ventilator machine standing beside the bed. Half expecting what he saw, John moved beyond the small toilet door and found Kimberley lying in the hospital bed. Eyes closed, the plastic pipes attached to the ventilator helped her to breathe, and John felt a surge of guilt as he looked down at her.

'This was your fault.' The Ripper's voice mocked from the walls once again. 'You led her right to me, and now I feed from her until she is of no use to me.'

John could see the colour draining from her youthful face as he looked down at her from the foot of the bed.

'This isn't her fight.' John snarled as his fingers gripped the rail at the end of the bed.

'You made it her fight.' The Ripper hushed, the voice almost in his ear, but John refused to tear his attention away from

Kimberley. 'Besides, by feeding from her slowly, I learn so much more about you.'

The words were enough to trigger him, and John span on the spot to find the room empty aside from him and Kimberley.

'Enough with the games.' John snapped as he ripped the mask from his face. 'Why not face me here and be done with it?'

'That would be too easy. We need you ready.'

'Ready for what?'

The Ripper attacked again and this time John was caught completely by surprise. Feeling the solid blow to his chest, he was powerless to resist the ferocious attack as he crash through the panoramic glass window on the far side of the room. Splinters of glass exploded in every direction as John caught sight of the Ripper standing at the foot of Kimberley's hospital bed. Unable to do anything but fall, John prepared himself for the inevitable collision with the floor and clamped his eyes shut. Although he knew there would be no pain, there would be the sense of defeat which felt even more painful at that moment.

Feeling nothing, John opened his eyes and found himself once again stood looking at the open door from Goulston Street. As the Victorian buildings once were replaced by the modern exteriors, John felt his heart sink. There was no sign of the hospital room of mocking face of the Ripper looking down at him from above. All there was, were the old windows of the buildings above the shopfront, offering him his only glimpse into a past that consumed his attention, yet seemed irrelevant to the sea of people who meandered the night streets.

Knowing he had something to go on, John turned his back on the doorway, which was the last thing to disappear from his memory view of Goulston Street. Desperate to leave the shadows behind, he once again moved through the sea of unconscious minds. The advantage of his shroud of death was the fact he could move without notice to most. Only when he consciously moved into the living realm could anyone see him, as had happened in Mitre Square, but for the rest of the time he move unseen by the masses.

Reveling in the anonymity it afforded him, John navigated the London streets with no sense of urgency. Although he could move with speed, a heavy shadow hung over his thoughts as he moved closer to the all-too-familiar hospital he had seen Kimberley in. St Thomas' Hospital was a place he had avoided, and it was no surprise the Ripper had somehow manufactured the circumstances to bring Kimberley into the confines of the hospital. An impressive structure in its day, the hospital had stood as a spired structure with a grand silhouette when it had first opened. Sat on the opposite banks as the Palace of Westminster, the architecture matched its grandiose surroundings, but now it stood a curious mix of old architecture and angular modern structures.

By the time John reached the hospital, his mind weighed heavily. Memories he had long since boxed away and ignored threatened to consume him as he admired the elegant spires and remnants of Victorian London standing tall before him. Knowing the room that called from his memories, John levelled his gaze at an innocuous glass-paned window high above. To anyone else there was nothing special about the window, it looked the same as all the others that surrounded it, but John knew different. To him, he could make out the familiar silhouette in the glass and quickly pulled his attention away from the haunting memory.

Not wishing or willing to dwell on the elements of his past he had buried, John made his way around the site and found his way into the newer wings, a place he had no connection with. It took a matter of moments to follow his senses and find the door to Kimberley's room. Pausing at the door, John struggled to make sense of the strange feelings that he felt. Albeit a sense of responsibility hung over him with Azrael's words, but there was something else behind all that. Shaking aside the confusion, John pushed open the door and stepped into the room.

Just as in the strange vision of the Ripper, the air was filled with the sound of medical machinery. A symphony of beeps accompanied the artificially supported inhale and exhale as the ventilator kept Kimberley alive. Moving into the room, John paused to take in the room and Kimberley's motionless form on the bed.

'What have I done to you?' John croaked as he moved to the panoramic window.

The glass framed Westminster and Big Ben and as the dawn sun crested behind the horizon, it bathed London in the eerie morning glow of the new sun. Watching the world come alive, John remained at the window and felt a sense of watchful patience. Stealing the moment as his own, he focussed on the rhythmic sounds of the machines and forced his mind to calm itself. In all that had happened in the days since his escape from the Nuthall Hospital, he had found himself thrust back into a world he had hidden from for almost four decades. Despite that fact, the world had welcomed him with open arms as if no time had passed at all. Laying his weapons on the windowsill, John threw his coat on the chair in the corner of the room and waited.

He needed time to think and to bring Kimberley back from wherever it was she had been taken.

22

KIMBERLEY'S MIND

J ohn remained in the room, a silent sentinel as the hospital
staff completed their checks on Kimberley. Unseen by the
nurses, John waited until they did the checks before moving
back to the side of Kimberley's bed.

'Where are you right now?' John hushed as he watched the
rhythmic movement of her chest as the ventilator helped her
breathe. 'How can I get you back from wherever you are?

Making sure they were alone, John pulled the seat from the
corner of the room and dropped to sit beside the bed. Watching
the dance of lines and readings on the screens, John fought
with himself on how to proceed. Seeing Kimberley's tranquil
expression on her face, there was no escaping the guilt that hung
in the air. He knew her current condition was solely down to
him. Cursing under his breath, John threw his head back and
looked up at the ceiling. Counting the holes in the dusty air
conditioning outlet, he accepted what he had to do and pressed
his palm to her forehead.

The moment his skin touched hers, he felt himself dragged from the bedside and back into the murky world of his memories. Aware of the disruption his last journey would have caused, John was careful to control his arrival as much as he could. As his surroundings built themselves around him, he struggled to place himself in any particular place or time. After what felt like an age, the tall Victorian buildings towered around him and the streets became familiar.

Little time had passed from the Mitre Square murders and, judging by the lightness of the pre-dawn clouds, the police would have found the chalk message and bloodstained apron in Goulston Street by now. Scanning around, John's attention fell to the familiar swinging sign for the pub. Marching his way across the street, the air was thick with smoke and filled with the chatter of voices despite the hour. Passing through the open door, John scanned the crowds of faces but saw no sign of Kimberley.

Checking the darkest corners of the busy pub, John turned to leave when something caught his attention. It wasn't Kimberley, but something that danced in the corner of his vision up on the stairs behind the bar. Moving through the crowd, John passed beside the unsuspecting bartender and climbed the rickety staircase up onto the next level of the building. As he reached the landing, the sounds of the voices from below grew muffled and indistinguishable. Glad for the quiet, John scanned both ways but saw nothing.

'Kimberley?' John was careful not to be too loud, not wanting to bring himself to the attention of his memories.

With no reply, he moved along the length of the dank hallway and reached a large window that overlooked the rear courtyard behind the pub. The courtyard was empty at first glance. Nothing moved amongst the barrels and piled boxes, but something looked out of place. Seeing something at odds with the Victorian gothic surrounded, John caught sight of a pair of trainers sat against one box.

Transporting himself into the courtyard, John recognised the trainers as Kimberley's.

'How long did it take you?' Kimberley spat as she lurched towards John.

Dressed in the clothes of the era, Kimberley looked different. Taken aback by the change in her appearance, John caught the frustrated clenched fist aimed squarely at his head. Deflecting her attack, he stepped back enough to give her space enough to prepare for a follow-up attack.

'I guess you adopted my manner of blending in?' John offered with a coy smile that seemed to infuriate her all the more.

'Didn't give me much choice, did you?' Kimberley spat as she surged forward again.

'Come now, you've only been here a couple of days.'

'Couple of days?' Kimberley snarled as John easily dodged her. 'I've lived the same day countless times.'

'Oh.'

'Sorry? Is that it?'

Distracted by the thought, Kimberley's next attack found its mark as she slammed a fist onto his right cheek. Surprised by the attack, John scooped his arms around her torso and pulled her close, stopping her from preparing to attack again. Gripping her tight, his face ended up next to hers so he could offer his reply as little more than a hushed whisper in her ear.

'I'm sorry.' John hissed. 'I didn't mean it to be like this.'

'Let me go.'

Ripping free of his grasp, Kimberley's dress floated in the air as she put space between them and glared at him in the dusky courtyard. Allowing her ragged breaths to settle, John took in her appearance and felt a wave of nostalgia. Kimberley, for however long she had been trapped in this memory, had done well to blend in with her surroundings. Wearing a long dress with her hair matching the style of the era, she would have stirred no attention from the memory's defences at her being an imposter, despite her footwear. Knowing it wasn't the time to celebrate her ingenuity, John admired how she had adapted.

'We need to get you out of here.' John offered his hand out to her.

'Where have you been?' Kimberley remained steadfast on the other side of the courtyard. 'Why didn't you come straight back in here and get me?'

'I didn't know where you were.' John confessed, dropping his open hand to his side.

'I'm inside your bloody head.' Kimberley snapped, barely controlling the anger boiling inside her. 'How can you not know where I am when I'm in your memories?'

'Because I didn't put you there.' John moved to sit on an overturned box. 'I'm still not sure how you came back to me here, I'm not even sure this is my memory.'

'Well, it's not mine, is it?'

'Obviously not. But you've adapted well enough to hide in plain sight.'

'They did not leave me with much choice. They hunted me every time they saw me, then I remembered what you said about the ripples. The only way that seemed to work was to act like one of them.' Kimberley found her own seat, still keeping a cautious distance from John. 'What makes you think this isn't your memory?'

'Because I don't recognise this place. I've been in the pub before but never here, never in the upper levels and yet they all felt familiar.'

'If they're not yours?'

'I'd rather not think about that right now.' John confessed as he looked around at the courtyard. 'Can you remember how you got here?'

'I thought this was the same place as before. You sent me here when you didn't want me near the Ripper thing.'

'Yes, but I never felt you arrive in my mind. It was like some-one hid you from me and it makes no sense. That's why I never for a moment thought I would find you here.'

'So how are you here if this isn't your memory?'

John took the time to explain how he had watched Kimberley flee Mitre Square as the overzealous police officers had dragged him into the back of the idling police car. As he recalled what he had seen, it was clear from the look on Kimberley's face she had no recollection of anything he was saying. Talking her through the days of searching for her, John left out his conversation with Azrael atop Tower Bridge and the fact it had reminded him of the precarious position he had put Kimberley in.

'You've still not answered how you're here if this place isn't inside your head.'

'I found you in St Thomas' Hospital.' John confessed, his voice struggling to grow louder than a whisper. 'I found you and connected with you. This is *your* memory.'

'It can't be. I've never been here before, except for when you sent me here.'

'Then the alternative is far more dangerous than I would like to admit and it's time we left.'

Seeing the look of concern on John's face, Kimberley rose from her makeshift seat and waited for him to join her. Taking one last look around, feeling he was somehow balanced on a knife-edge for some inexplicable reason, John moved to join Kimberley and removed the leather glove from his hand. Holding out his hand, he waited for Kimberley to reach for him. As she did, the air grew colder and as their skin was about to touch and all too familiar voice boomed from the shadows.

'That isn't your way out of here.' The Ripper's sinister voice heckled from behind the wooden fence.

Hearing the steady footfalls, John moved Kimberley behind him and recalled the plague doctor mask to his face. Sensing the demon's presence, both of them followed the sound of footsteps until the Ripper moved into the open gateway on the far side of the courtyard. Bathed in the eerie dusk shadows, neither of them could make out the Ripper's features, but neither could deny his physical presence as he stepped through the gateway.

The deep shadow cast by the top hat kept its face from view but they could see the sinister, smouldering eyes that glared at them. Almost nonchalantly, the Ripper placed its hands in its pockets and waited for one of them to speak.

'What is this place?' John pressed, already knowing the answer.

'Dear boy, you can't claim to be so ignorant in this mess. If you are, then I think your master should have chosen a better candidate.'

'This is yours.' It wasn't a question, more a defeated acceptance of what he had already realised. 'Your echo, how we found you in Mitre Square. We weren't free when I pushed Kimberley away.'

'Maybe Azrael didn't make a mistake.' The Ripper mocked. 'You sent her to me on a plate and with it, you've given me the key to everything I need to know about you.'

'You need to run.' Turning his back on the Ripper, John took hold of Kimberley and forced her to look at him.

'I need to get out of here.' Kimberley's face was awash with panic.

'I'll come back for you, I promise.'

'How long?'

'I don't know.'

'Don't leave me. Please.'

'I can't just take you from here. If this is his memory, then he holds the key to your escape. I'll help you, I promise, but I can't do that from in here.' John could see the terror in her eyes. 'Now, run.'

Pushing her away, John turned his back to avoid seeing the look of terror on her face. Casting aside the ridiculous sense of guilt, John returned his attention to the Ripper. Grateful to hear Kimberley making her escape, John withdrew the escrima sticks.

'I'm not here for a fight.' The Ripper replied, unmoved by the threat John offered.

'So, what do you want?'

'Despite your charm, that's not something we are willing to discuss.' The Ripper mocked as he turned to leave. 'You'll do well to forget your ward. She's mine now and we both know she can't leave until I'm done with her.'

'You're not having her.'

'I already have her mind.' The Ripper boomed as he stalked away. 'Soon enough, I will consume her soul exactly as I have the others, and you only have yourself to blame for this one.'

John launched at the Ripper, both weapons held in front of him, and pounced. Diving across the courtyard, John passed through the Ripper. Instead of crashing to the floor, John launched up and away from Kimberley's bedside as the world span around him. Ripping the mask from his face, he realised he had not had it on when he had entered Kimberley's mind and scanned the room for any sign of the Ripper. Realising they were still alone, John looked down at Kimberley and saw a solitary tear staining the side of her face.

Cursing under his breath, John moved to the large window and stared out across the turbulent water of the Thames, lost in his thoughts. Dropping his gaze to the windowsill, John's attention fell to a newspaper that had been left. Seeing the headline, he realised it must have been left by the previous occupant of the hospital room. Emblazoned on the front page was the familiar scene of Mitre Square, awash with police officers and a large forensic tent where the woman's body had been. Unfolding the newspaper, John smoothed out the crumpled image and stared at the carnage his fight with the Imps had left behind.

Pushing the newspaper away, John turned to offer Kimberley one last promise.

'I know you can hear me.' John hushed as he moved to her bedside. 'Find your way out of there and I'll do what I can from here. Somewhere we will be in the same place and I'll bring you back, but first I need to find him.'

Composing himself, John made sure his presence was shielded and moved to the door. Moving into the corridor, he left Kimberley with one last thought.

'I promise I'm not leaving you.'

With nothing left to say, John disappeared, leaving the room quiet once again save for the rhythmic movements of the ventilator that kept Kimberley alive.

23

THE MAGIC CIRCLE

Having left the hospital, John made his way to Mitre Square. Frustrated by the way in which this had all played out, he could not shake the feeling he had lost control. Having believed the Ripper had been banished, John had always wondered why his death had never been honoured. His time between facing the Ripper and surrendering his freedom to the Nuthall Hospital had been as a lost warrior, without a sense of reason or purpose. In all of his years confined and contained, it had never crossed his mind that the Ripper had survived.

Directing himself away from Mitre Square, he instead brought himself to Hyde Park and found himself standing in front of the impressive structure of the Old Police House. While the building itself hadn't changed over the years, the shrubbery and foliage had. The frontage of the building remained clear and well-pruned, and yet the sides were now shielded by walls of trees, shrubs, and plants. Avoiding the heavy wooden door that sat dead centre of the building's front, John moved around to the side and searched through the shrubbery.

Although the main building spanned over three floors, the side aspects only occupied two levels. With most of the windows concealed behind the greenery, John was not as concerned about his visibility as he pulled aside roots and branches in search of a small stone statue. Finding nothing, the frustration rose until at last his hands found what he was looking for. Ripping away the entwined ivy that had buried the old stone gargoyle, John took a moment to admire the craftmanship.

Perched on a stone plinth, the gargoyle looked like it belong on the side of an old church spire somewhere, not beside a police station in the beating heart of a royal garden. It had been an addition of John's design almost half a century before and had indeed come from the face of Westminster Abbey when the Ripper and Raven had faced on another on the dark, stormy night of the Ripper's believed end.

'Nothing like a demon from your past to destroy everything.' John muttered as he caressed the stone gargoyle's head. 'I guess there's only one way to know for sure.'

Speaking only to himself, John stroked the weathered head of the gargoyle until his fingers found the concealed recess between the oversized ears. Pressing down, he made sure nobody else was watching and waited. The mechanisms that secured the subterranean tomb had not moved in decades and he feared the hidden entrance would not open. After what felt like an age, the ground shook beneath his feet and the ground moved aside, allowing him access to a narrow staircase leading beneath the Old Police Station building. Wasting no time, knowing the entrance could be seen, even if he could not, John dropped into the opening and pulled the heavy stone back behind him.

Swallowed by the darkness, John allowed his eyes to settle and descended the staircase. Unbeknown to the workers and inhabitants of the Old Police Station, the underground tomb had never been discovered. Concealed for centuries, John had learned of its existence from Azrael when he had sought a way to banish the Ripper from existence. The tomb was one of many locations where a demon soul could be trapped and finally snuffed out of existence.

Each tomb contained a single stone coffin emblazoned with symbols and writings John had never understood. The stormy night that John had finally faced the Ripper, it had all led here. Even walking down the winding staircase, he could almost feel the Ripper behind him. That night, the ceilings had dripped with rainwater and John had dragged the bound and battered Ripper behind him down into the main room.

Built on the ancient Mesopotamian ritual of Zissuru, the tomb was, in essence, a reverse of the protective spell that kept demons from infecting the living. Once a demon was brought into the confines of the tomb, they were incapable of escaping, even more so when placed inside the stone coffin. The same enchantments and dark magic trapped them inside and drained what little life was stolen inside them.

As he reached the bottom of the steps, John found it difficult to differentiate the here and now from the flashing images of his memories. The only other time he had been in the Zissuru was to banish the Ripper into the very stone coffin that sat in the centre of the circular room. Stopping dead in his tracks, John was overcome with panic as the room was now nothing more than an empty tomb, only the damaged stone remained in the floor where the coffin had once stood.

Not having known what to expect, in some way hoping the flashes of the Ripper were nothing more than invading memories, John had not expected the coffin to be gone. Entering the Zissuru, he had expected to find the stone lid removed somehow and nothing more than a vacant coffin in the wake of the Ripper's escape. Still struggling to piece together *how* the Ripper had been freed, the lack of any stone confused him all the more. Stomping across to the four shattered supports on the ground, John inspected the damage and scanned for any sign of what had happened in the dark tomb.

Admiring the moss-covered walls, John could still make out some inscriptions etched into the stone. Constellations adorned the ceilings and where roots had traced through the narrow cracks, the entire room felt alive. What had once been a sealed sanctuary now felt nothing more than an abandoned relic with little purpose left. Frustrated by the riddle of what had happened, John moved back to the stairs and made his way back to ground level. Activating the hidden switch to open the door, he made sure the entrance remained unseen before destroying the mounted gargoyle.

'No point in having it found.' John scoffed as he dropped the shattered stone face and pressed into the mud with his feet.

Moving back through Hyde Park, John struggled to find a coherent thought as he made his way back towards his original destination. Wandering the streets rather than calling on his gift to move with haste, he admired the diversity of London as it was. Passing by groups of tourists from every corner of the world, John couldn't help but feel a sense of pride at what the grand capital had become. Although many of the buildings were as he remembered, the beating heart of the city had changed in so many ways that he hardly recognised it anymore.

Arriving at Mitre Square, it didn't surprise him to find the scene alive with police. Uniformed constables guarded every entrance to the square while two smartly dressed women were held in conversation with a gaggle of figures dressed in white forensic suits. Although the method of their investigations was beyond John's limited understanding, he knew the investigation was till in its infancy, if only by the sheer number of people gathered around the tent where the poor woman's body still remained.

Observing from the shadows of the alleyway, John listened to the hushed conversation between the two officers stationed on the other side of the flapping crime scene tape. Ever cautious to remain on the periphery of their consciousness, he pressed closer in the hope the conversation would give him something to go on. Having thought about the pattern of attacks, this was not the same as the Ripper's previous exploits, a fact that had not escaped him.

'Did you hear what they'd done to her?'

'I heard they'd gutted her. What sick bastard does that to a woman?'

'They keep saying it's a copycat killer.'

'Yeah, but how does he keep getting away?' The officer checked they were not being overheard. 'Colin said he was reviewing the CCTV and it was like, well, she did it to herself.'

'No chance can anyone do that to themselves.'

'Mate, there was nobody on the camera, nothing.'

'I've never seen London like this. Even the gangsters are scared. I tell you one thing, if someone else catches whoever this is, they'll not be brought to us alive.'

'Yeah, nothing like a serial killer to light the fires.'

Having heard enough, John ducked beneath the tape and moved past the two officers unseen. Careful to remain purposeful in his movements, John navigated the crime scene and looked for any signs of the Imps that had attacked him from the rooftops. Seeing nothing, John tuned his senses to the unseen marks and immediately they were revealed to him. Where had had fought back the onslaught of winged creatures, the ground was pitted and scorched, a telltale sign of demonic possession. Following the trail across the tarmac and over the front of the building, John stopped in his tracks as a sudden movement stole his attention.

High above on the rooftop, John was sure he had seen something move. Too big to be a bird, he wasn't sure, but the sudden sense of fear told him it was the Ripper. Wasting no time, John projected himself onto the rooftop and prepared himself for a fight.

Arriving amongst the air conditioning units and heavy industrial cabling, John found himself alone on the roof. Seeing no echo of the Ripper, John searched the length and breadth of the building and found nothing. Knowing what he had sensed, John moved the roof's edge and looked down at the square from where he had seen the shadow of the Ripper. Still experiencing the world through his heightened senses, he realised what he had been missing from ground level.

The demon scorch marks that littered the ground had appeared as chaotic remnants of a furious battle. From his perch above, he could now see them for what they were. Viewed from a bird's-eye perspective, John could now see a symbol scorched into the ground, a symbol he had not seen for many years. The pattern made out two crescent moons, one on its end with the other seated on the fine point of the other. Two lines cut through the lower moon and John realised all points were directed towards the tent and the dead woman's body.

'Hey, you.' A voice bellowed from below and John stepped back from the roof's edge, fearing he had been seen.

Looking around, John felt a wave of relief as he caught sight of a terrified young man with an array of cameras attached to his neck. Grateful for the distraction of the reporter, John watched as the police all but emptied the square to apprehend the wayward reporter on the adjacent rooftop. Grateful for the distraction, John dropped from the roof, landing with impressive grace, and walked across Mitre Square and into the oversized forensic tent that shrouded the mutilated body from view.

'My apologies for not protecting you from the darkness.' John offered as he stopped above the woman's body.

To his relief, she remained concealed beneath a black sheet, her vicious wounds no longer visible. Taking a moment, John dropped to his knees and pulled the top of the sheet back to expose the young woman's lifeless face. Cold air was being pumped into the forensic tent in an attempt to keep the body from decaying. It was not an investigative tactic John was familiar with, but he was grateful the body remained in the same position, it would make what he now had to do a little easier to achieve.

'Forgive me,' John offered as he removed his gloves and pressed his hands to both sides of the dead woman's head. 'But I must ask you something.'

Despite the grey, lifeless skin, the woman's face twitched at his touch. Calling all his strength, John called the woman's soul back and watched as the dead face returned to life.

'Where am I?' She stammered, her milky eyes blinking away the blindness of death.

'You have nothing to fear. I need only to speak with you briefly.'

'Why can't I see? Where am I?' The questions poured from her cracked lips, but John didn't have time to settle the wayward soul's fears.

'I am The Raven, Death's Hand and I seek a way to find the thing that did this to you.'

'It was so fast, I didn't know what had happened.'

'How did you come to be here?'

'I was meeting someone.'

'Who?'

'For business, for work. They paid me to meet him. They were going to pick me up.'

'What business?'

'Please, I don't want to be dead. Is there anything you can do?'

John hated what he was doing. Bringing a passing soul back to its body was something that weighed heavily on him. Knowing the woman would already be in turmoil, existing in the world between life and death awaiting judgement, he knew the damage such a connection could cause. Not wanting to keep her any longer, John saw her milky eyes were clearing. He was running out of time.

'There's nothing I can do for you now. That moment has passed.' John fought to keep her attention fixed on him as he knew the world would be coming into focus for her. 'Who were you supposed to meet?'

'They always use fake names. Nobody wants to give their real name to a hooker.' The woman fought against his grip as she tried to take in her surroundings.

'What name did he give you?'

'They said I was to meet John Smith, not an original name, I know.' Realising this was nothing more than another layer to the Ripper's game, John knew this was a fruitless venture.

Seeing the woman's eyes drop to the now exposed torso, John ended his connection and watched as the soul once again left the woman's body. Awash with guilt, John wasted no more time with the mutilated corpse and faded away before the square was once again occupied.

24

— • —

THE RITUAL

'I'm with her now, but there's no sign of him.' Diana's voice carried in from the corridor as she peered through the door to Kimberley's room. 'Yes, I am sure.'

The voice on the other end of the phone was muffled, their words unclear, but the expression on Diana's face said enough. Seeing his rising frustration, she offered no more replies and simply ended the call. Sliding the phone back into her pocket, she checked she was alone in the hospital corridor and stepped into the room, closing the door behind her.

'You're a difficult one to find, all things considered.' Diana hushed as she moved across the room and sat in the same chair John had occupied hours before. 'I was hoping our mutual friend would be here, but I guess not.'

Pulling the clipboard from the end of the bed, Diana scanned the printed sheets and perused the results as if she knew what they meant. Making no sense of the rough scrawls of black ink on the various sheets, Diana tossed the clipboard onto the bottom of the bed and leant back in the chair. Drinking in

Kimberley's appearance, she took a moment to admire the myriad of tubes and cables that fed from the various machines to Kimberley's body beneath the thin sheets.

'I know you can hear me.' Diana hissed as she watched the ventilator feeding Kimberley oxygen. 'This isn't what the doctors think it is. This is no coma. You're simply dying, my dear.'

To anyone wondering past the room, it would seem like nothing more than a loved one offering comfort in times of distress. Without hearing the almost monologue explanation, Diana's interaction was entirely normal.

'The Ripper is feeding from you. Taking what insignificant life is left in you, and we both know who can stop it.' Diana leaned in closer. 'You can call him back to you. You know you can.'

There was the slightest of twitches, the smallest movement in Kimberley's face, that told Diana she was listening. Holding back the surge of excitement, she placed her hand on Kimberley's and continued to speak.

'Your pleas will bring him back to you. He will not turn his back on you, again.' Her voice was seductive and laced with suggestion. 'It's a simple request. Ask him to help you, not leave you alone in the darkness.'

Reaching into her bag, Diana removed a curious leather bundle and opened it up on the windowsill.

'I need him here, to end all of this and bring about the prophecy of our order.' Diana spoke as she removed the items from the bundle and laid them out around the room.

Lighting a dark candle, she placed the flickering flame on the windowsill and closed the heavy curtains. Plunging the room into darkness, the only light came from the dancing candlelight as she moved around the room like a spectral silhouette. Placing similar candles in all four corners of the room, Diana returned to the bedside and wheeled the table across so she could spread out the remaining items.

'In this world of technology, it is sometimes the rituals of old that bring us what we need.' Diana explained to the motionless Kimberley as she allowed her eyes to adjust to the dim light in the room. 'Everything has led to this moment. I need you to know how instrumental you were in all of this. Without you, none of this would have been possible.'

Almost perversely, Diana moved a strand of hair from Kimberley's face as she lay unmoving on the bed. There was almost an intimacy in the way she looked down at the unconscious younger woman.

'You are our path to the prophecy.' Diana whispered into Kimberley's ear before lighting the final candle and placing it on the table above her torso.

The room was awash with dancing shadows as the candles stirred in an unfelt breeze. Removing her jacket, Diana rolled up her sleeves and unfolded a piece of discoloured parchment beside the candle on the table. Adorned with the same obscure symbols and images, she flattened out the sheet before closing her eyes and beginning whatever ritual it was she was about to perform.

'A burnt jewel. A hell demons throne.' Diana recited the prophecy of the Full Moon Society, but it was not her voice that finished it.

'Both twins will meet a fight.'

The second voice was deeper and sinister. Turning her attention to the darkest corner of the room, Diana watched as the Ripper peeled itself from the shadow and sauntered towards her. Every shadow felt like it was connected to the dark creature as it removed its top hat. Every ounce of the predator it was, Diana was grateful for the dimness of the candlelight as it masked most of the discoloured and terrifying features of the demonic monster before her.

'The ritual has begun.' Diana announced, clearing the croak in her voice with a sharp cough. 'He will be here.'

'Good.' Retreating back into the shadows, the only sign he remained were the pale whites of his eyes watching as Diana continued her ritual.

The shadows grew darker as Diana recited the words, spoken in an unrecognisable, ancient tongue. Growing outwards from the Ripper's corner, the shadows looked as roots growing away from the hovering pale eyes, reaching ever closer to Kimberley. As the candles continued to flicker, Diana's words became faster and more indistinguishable. At last the feeling in the room changed and where the shadows almost touched Kimberley's pale skin, they now stopped moving.

'She is not yours.' John's familiar voice boomed as he appeared by Kimberley's bedside.

Dressed in his garb as the Raven, the plague doctor mask concealed his face but his voice was immediately recognisable. Glancing down at Kimberley, John once again saw the slightest signs of movement on her face but quickly returned his attention to Diana.

'She's not yours either.' Diana hissed as she stepped away from the hospital bed, snatching the discoloured parchment as she moved.

'I expected better.' John growled as he swiped his arm across the rolling table, spilling the contents to the floor.

'As did I.'

John was about to strike when his senses warned him of the Ripper's presence. Having been scouring the London streets for signs of his adversary, John had felt Kimberley's call and answered. Transporting himself back into the familiar hospital room, the sight that had greeted him was not what he had expected. Seeing Diana poised above the hospital bed and the flickering Demon-Candles within the room, he had sensed the presence of darkness but attributed it to Diana. It was only as she backed away that he saw the shadows draw and the silhouette of the Ripper against the surrounding darkness.

'All you had to do was ask.' John barked as he ripped the escrima sticks from his back. 'Rather than hiding in the shadows and playing games.'

'And miss the fun of your failed attempts to locate me in a city of millions?' The Ripper mocked as he pulled up the collar of his charred coat. 'All that hard work and it took the painful cries of a woman to bring you to me.'

'The misery you've left behind is hardly something to smirk about.'

'Needs must, to stay alive.'

John had heard enough. Unwilling to accept any more of the Ripper's disregard for life, he launched over Kimberley's bed and attacked. Knocking Diana aside, sending her crashing to the ground, John paid no attention to the Ripper's puppet and focussed his attention on his adversary. Crashing into the powerful demon, John hammered a series of attacks on the Ripper until they slammed into the far wall where he had been hiding. Pressing his masked face close to the Ripper's, John offered his words so only they could hear.

'You're not having her.'

'I already have.' The Ripper snarled, revealing a mouth full of jagged teeth. 'And she's tasted oh so good.'

Knowing the fact the Ripper was provoking him, John disregarded it and unleashed his full fury on him. Slamming his fist into the Ripper, the demon accepted each blow with little reaction until, after what felt like an age, the Ripper caught John's fist in his hand. Not uttering a word, he lifted John from the ground and in one swift movement, the Ripper threw him across the room, sending him crashing through the Victorian window of the hospital room. Shards of glass sprayed over Kimberley's motionless form on the bed as daylight streamed in through the shattered window and torn curtains.

'Here, take this for me.' The Ripper offered as he tossed the burnt top hat at Diana.

Bathed in the bright sunlight, the Ripper's full form came into view. The clothes he wore reflected his origins in the eighteen-hundreds and yet looked burned and charred. Tailored to contain his muscular frame, the features of his face were a perfect fusion of human and demon. Blood-red eyes looked out from the deep recesses of his face and what at first appeared to be smoothed hair was in fact, two crooked horns that sat neatly swept back over his head and down his neck. Flattening his collar, the Ripper launched himself out of the window and disappeared from the room.

Watching The Ripper disappear, Diana stared at the scorched hat in her hand. Exhausted from the incoherent incantations, her attention fell to the floor as she scanned for the demon-faced coin she had laid on the table as she had begun the ritual. Seeing the coin under Kimberley's bed, she let go of the Ripper's hat and reached under the bed to retrieve the coin.

'What's happening?' Kimberley croaked from above on the bed as Diana snatched up the coin. 'Where am I?'

Doing her best to appear calm, Diana moved along the length of the bed and rose with her back to the disorientated young woman.

'Doctor will be with you in a minute.' Diana offered in a quiet voice, fighting to hide her identity.

'Where am I?'

'Hospital, I'll go get the doctor for you.'

Gathering her things, not wanting Kimberley to see her face, Diana left the smouldering candles in the corners of the room and made her way to the door. Keeping her back to the hospital bed, Diana made her exit and left the room. As the door close, Diana caught sight of Kimberley as she set about pulling the various tubes and cables from her arms and legs, sending the machines into a chorus of screeching alarms. Seeing the nurses come running towards the flashing light above Kimberley's door, Diana made her way in the opposite direction and disappeared from view. Melting into the anonymity of the busy hospital, she made her exit and left the chaos of what had happened behind her.

Only once she was out of view, confined to the empty staircase, Diana took a moment to catch her breath and steady her shaking hands. Although she had been aware of what would happen with the summoning of the Raven, she had not known the reaction it would bring. Although he had been masked, the contempt he had for the Ripper had been tangible in the air and, in that moment, Diana realised that hatred was far more powerful than she had expected. Seeing the ferocity of John's attacks, she had worried for the Ripper's ability to defeat Death's Hand.

Hearing a fresh chorus of panic and screams from somewhere within the hospital, Diana knew it was time to leave.'

25

BATTLE OF AGES

What unfolded outside the shattered hospital window went unseen by those on the streets below. United in their desire to remain invisible to the world, both John and the Ripper shrouded their presence. That said, as Diana burst through the open door, she was conscious enough to see the two of them standing on the face of the old hospital building, using it as their floor as they fought between themselves. Defying gravity as they moved along the building, it was obvious the scream had come from the floor below where another window had shattered in the time it had taken her to navigate the labyrinth of corridors within the hospital.

'What's done is done. Fate will decide. Now come.' Qamar's familiar voice announced from the open window of the idling SUV.

Unseen by the battling duo, Diana clambered into the vehicle and disappeared into the flow of traffic. Concerned only with the fight before him, John had shrugged free of his coat and now moved with unhindered speed along the front of the old hospital. Using the window frames and sills as purchase, John kept his focus on the Ripper through the lenses of his mask and released a flurry of attacks that kept the Ripper moving back along the building.

Using his own weapons, the Ripper wielded a pair of Liston knives as his weapons, a fact not lost on John as he expertly dodged the counter-attacks from his opponent. Knowing the mystery that surrounded the Ripper's original murder spree, John had pored over the news articles and police reports of which most pointed to a living man being responsible for them. It had only been in secret documentation that the idea of the Ripper being *something else* had surfaced, a theory eagerly buried and diverted from mainstream narratives.

John even recalled the first time the neat cuts created by the Ripper's own hands had been written off as the expert dissection skills of a madman armed with surgical knives. The same ones the Ripper now wielded as weapons to fight against him.

'You're woman has shared with me all the memories you gave to her.' The Ripper taunted as he dragged the blade dangerously close to John's masked face. 'I've seen your past and the shadows that haunt it.'

'Should be nothing new to you!' John retorted as he dropped a level and propelled himself back up towards the Ripper.

Dragging the escrima stick between his legs, John stole the Ripper's balance and sent them both crashing down to the grass below.

Precariously balanced between the realms of visible and unseen, John and The Ripper crashed over the railings and onto
the street beyond. As furiously as they fought, neither of them
found an advantage over the other. Their skills were matched
and yet John knew The Ripper was holding back. Knowing
the skills the demon possessed, John was aware that there was
something different about The Ripper's style and movements.
When they had last fought, his opponent had stalked like a
hunting tiger, relentless and ferocious in every movement. Now,
as he observed the demon's movements, there wasn't the same
ferocity in his fight.

Distracted by the thoughts, John dived back in time to see
the blade of the Liston knife pass in front of his face where his
head had been a split second before. Cursing his distraction,
John attempted to retaliate but found the space in front of him
devoid of The Ripper.

Scanning in all directions, John could see no sign of The
Ripper, only the remnants of the creature's echo. Snatching his
hand into the tendrils of smoke, John propelled himself along
The Ripper's line and followed him through. Dragged from the
roadside outside St Thomas' Hospital, John watched the world
blur around him as he travelled the lines between life and death.

Knowing The Ripper would expect his arrival, John prepared
himself for a fight as he saw his destination take shape in front of
him. Despite all his years of experiencing the turbulent journey
along the lines, his senses had no time to take in his surroundings as the spinning world settled and The Ripper attacked.

Slamming its fist into the back of John's masked head, he felt himself thrown to the grassy ground that absorbed most of his fall. Giving no element of respite, The Ripper was on him in a heartbeat and rained down a flurry of blows, forcing him to shield his face.

Fighting to make sense of his surroundings and keep himself from being pummelled into the ground by the powerful attacks, John stared through the lenses of his mask at the surrounding greenery. Unable to place where they had travelled to, John felt The Ripper's knife glide across his forearm and felt the sting of pain from the enchanted blade. Knowing he was at a tremendous disadvantage, John timed himself and caught the blade in his hand as The Ripper drove it down towards his face.

The tip of the quivering blade came to rest against the leather mask as John gripped the blade and held it back. While the knife appeared to be a mortal weapon, it was far from such a simple thing. Enchanted by the same dark magic that fed The Ripper and kept its presence in the living realm, John knew the blade was a significant threat. Feeling The Ripper press its weight onto the weapon, the tip pierced the leather and a fresh wave of panic washed over him.

For all his strength, the sheer power and weight of The Ripper was more than John could hold back. Digging his heels into the damp grass, he turned his head to the side to avoid the shimmering blade. As the Liston knife carved a neat hole along the length of his mask, John released the tension enough to force The Ripper to surge forward. Propelled by his own effort, the knife scraped across the copper detailing and sank into the damp ground by the side of John's head. Taking advantage of the distraction, John drove his knees up and launched the bulbous Ripper up and over his head.

Wasting no time, John crawled across the grass and snatched up one of the discarded escrima sticks and turned back to face his snarling opponent. Realising the plague doctor mask had been carved open, John ripped it from his face and dropped it to the ground by his feet.

'At last I get to see the fear in your eyes.' The Ripper beamed as he ripped the knife from the mud.

'I feared you many years ago, less so now.'

'Tell your eyes that.' The Ripper chuckled. 'I see far more fear than you let show. Your years in captivity have certainly eroded the warrior you once were.'

'And years in the ground have done little for your dashing good looks.'

Knowing they were both buying time, John took advantage of the distraction and realised they were once again standing in Hyde Park a short distance from the Old Police Station. Whether by chance or design, The Ripper's destination had brought them to the one place where John could trap the demon soul. Unsure why The Ripper had chosen this location, John spent no more time contemplating the reasons, and attacked.

The park was almost empty. The heavy grey clouds that released a downpour of rain was doing enough to keep most people inside. Ignoring the rain, John grasped the only escrima stick in one hand and set about doing his best to direct their fight towards the impressive structure that dominated the far side of the grass. If it could have been seen by the few that braved the weather, the fight between the pair would have looked like some ancient battle. Attacks were rough, aggressive, and filled with the sole intention of destroying their opponent. There was nothing graceful about their movements and attacks.

For every attack, a block and parry was waiting until neither of them had found leverage over the other. Catching The Ripper's next thrust, John used his strength to lift the hulky figure high into the air above the park and turned him over. Once The Ripper was beneath him, John allowed gravity to take its hold and drag them back down towards the ground. Keeping his position atop The Ripper, the pair slammed into the ground and John kept his weight on The Ripper's barreled chest.

The height of their fall and combined weight forced the sodden ground to absorb their impact, and it threw both of them in opposing directions under a shower of mud and turf. Rolling away over his shoulder, John fought to keep himself upright as The Ripper rolled across the grass end over end. Steadying himself, John sprinted across the grass and dived towards The Ripper as it crashed into a tree trunk beside the footpath.

John's attack had been ill-timed, and The Ripper was ready for him. Sensing what was coming, he gripped the Liston knife in his hand and thrust out the blade as John jumped into the air to deliver his attack. Catching sight of the glinting blade at the last minute, all John could do was make sure he positioned his body enough to keep the knife from finding its mark on his unmoving heart.

As he crashed into The Ripper, John immediately felt the sting of pain as the Liston knife pierced through his clothes and buried to the hand line the left side of his chest. Ignoring the fire that burned across the left side of his body, John tried to pull himself away but The Ripper had wrapped its powerful arm around his torso and pulled him close.

Held face-to-face with the demon, John saw every inch of detail on the demon's scarred face. Blackened and discoloured skin rippled as it spoke, and John felt his attention fall to the lifeless eyes that stared at him. Even this close, it was impossible to tell if the discoloured flesh was due to decay or the fact The Ripper had been born of brimstone and fire.

'Nothing like The Raven I expected, or deserve.'

Before John could offer any pithy remark or reply, The Ripper hoisted him into the air and, in one swift movement, threw him through the air towards the Old Police Station. Feeling the knife slip free from his chest, the pain remained as John flew towards the brick walls. Colliding with the weathered brick, it did nothing to absorb his momentum as John crashed through the wall, sending brick and mortar flying in every direction.

Collapsing to the floor beneath the rubble, an enormous section of the wall caved in on top of him and immediately the air was filled with the piercing shrill of an alarm. Buried under the rubble, John struggled to break free as he saw The

Ripper marching towards him through a narrow gap in the bricks. Hearing voices, John knew his shroud of secrecy would have slipped and both of them would be in full view of anyone investigating the sudden explosion that had rocked the building.

Rising from the pile of debris, John brushed himself off as a handful of startled police officers came running into the cell block. Realising bars surrounded him, John had come to rest in what had once been a holding cell. Looking to his side, he caught sight of a terrified bedraggled man pressed against the far side of his own cell.

'What are you?' The drunk man stammered as he looked wide-eyed at John.

'Avon calling.' He replied with a wry smile and returned his attention to The Ripper.

'Hey, you. Stay where you are.' An officer bellowed, coughing back the cloud of dust that filled the cell block.

'I'd leave that locked if I were you.' John offered as he moved to the gaping hole in the wall. 'I take it you can see the massive bloke stamping towards me?'

'Listen, just do as you're told.'

'Right, I'll wait here and let the nasty demon rip your souls out and use you as his starter, shall I?'

To emphasise his point, more out of a need for humour in a moment that had him feeling on the back foot, John moved to lean against the crumbled wall, allowing the officers a clear view of The Ripper.

'What is that?' The officer choked as he let go of the keys. 'What are you?'

'He's The Ripper.' John snarled as he manifested a new plague doctor mask on his face. 'And me dear boy, I'm The Raven!'

Leaping back out into the rain, John could feel all eyes watching him as he moved to meet The Ripper on the sodden lawn.

26

— · —

ERODED STRENGTH

The two of them collided on the footpath that ran alongside the now shattered wall of the Old Police Station. Immediately, John felt The Ripper's arms wrap around his waist and drive him up into the air before crashing him hard onto the concrete path. Both of them were disarmed, their weapons somewhere on the sodden grass and lost amongst the rubble. Their fight was much more physical and dirty.

Fighting against The Rippers vice-like grip, John forced his way out of the bear hug and raised his guard before delivering a trio of precisely aimed blows at The Ripper's head. Finding his target with each blow, John saw The Ripper take to the defence. With the escrima sticks or Liston knives, the two creatures were forced to spar in the hammering rain.

Feigning another blow, John dropped his shoulder and delivered a solid uppercut that lifted The Ripper onto his tiptoes. Sensing his advantage, John followed this with another blow and a third before The Ripper gained enough sense to block his incoming attack. Finding his path blocked, John felt like he had just punched a solid wall as his fist bounced off The Ripper's bulging shoulder. Stunned, John saw The Ripper's movement and braced himself for the return attack.

Under the disbelieving gaze of the police officers and quivering prisoner, they could only watch as the masked Raven and dark being of The Ripper fought on the wet grass. It was impossible to see who had leverage over the other as blows were delivered and blocked with impossible speed and strength. From the onlookers, John's masked appearance seemed tame compared to the distorted and discoloured appearance of The Ripper.

From the side-lines, viewed through the jagged hole in the brick wall, all eyes were locked on the battling warriors. As John lost his footing on the grass, he was once again thrown through the air by a solid attack from The Ripper and came to rest against the pile of shattered bricks. Shaking off the attack, The Ripper sprinted towards him and John could only brace himself as his opponent delivered a solid kick into his chest.

Grateful for the fact there was no air in his lungs, John caught the second kick and sent The Ripper tumbling to the rubble. Taking their fight to the ground, the pair rolled into the vacant cell and crashed against the solid bars. Landing on top of The Ripper, John took hold of his head and slammed it into the bars. Despite the sheer amount of punches and blows he delivered, The Ripper showed no sign the attacks were even phasing him.

Terrified by what they were seeing, the officers had backed away from the cell and in their wake, John found an extendable baton discarded on the other side of the bars. Reaching through, The Ripper took the advantage and pushed John to the side. The sickening sound of breaking bone sounded in the air and even one officer yelped in response. With his arm at an awkward angle, John showed no sign of pain or even care that his arm was broken.

Unphased by the sound of snapping bone, John landed roughly against the bars and kicked out to keep The Ripper from diving on top of him. Despite his broken arm, John snatched the baton and pulled his arm back through the bars. Much to the horror of all those watching, John flexed his arm and snapped it back into its natural position as if nothing had happened. Extending the baton as he attacked, John drove the metal bar through the air and smashed it into the side of The Ripper's head with tremendous force.

Flinching against the blow, John seized the opportunity and dragged the baton across The Ripper's throat and moved behind to trap his head against his torso. Squeezing with all his strength, The Ripper dragged its jagged nails across John's arms and back in an attempt to break free of his crushing grasp but John refused to budge. Gripping the baton on both hands, John screamed with effort as he tried to break The Ripper's neck.

'You know this is futile.' The Ripper gargled as the baton crushed his windpipe. 'Nothing you do to me here, can stop me.'

'We've danced this merry dance before, you know there are ways.' John growled through the leather mask.

'That was then. This is now.'

Finding purchase, The Ripper lifted, forcing John back against the bars. Pressed against the metal, neither of them budged and were equally matched in strength and determination.

'Must we do this?' The Ripper choked.

Slamming his head back, The Ripper smashed into the mask and for a split second John's grip weakened. It was all he needed and in a heartbeat, John found the tables turned and The Ripper span around to face him. Face-to-face The Ripper released an unearthly growl that rattled inside John's mask. Opening its jaw wider than humanly possible, dislocating the lower jaw, John saw rows of razor-sharp teeth as The Ripper transformed into the true demon it was.

Growing in size, John could not keep his grip on the baton and felt himself pressed harder against the bars as The Ripper's bulk almost doubled in size. Using the blunt top of the baton, John drove the metal end into The Ripper's right eye and buried it as far as he could into his head, hearing the sickening *squelch* as the eyeball was crushed by the chrome shaft.

Staggering backwards, John was freed from the crushing press against the metal bars and dropped to his knees. Clutching at his chest, John saw The Ripper flailing to rip the baton free from his skull and made his move. Tackling The Ripper around his waist, John realised how much larger and bulkier The Ripper now was. Unbalanced by John's surprise attack, The Ripper fought to keep himself upright as they barrelled out of the jagged opening and crashed into the outside wall of the Old Police Station.

Bouncing along the wall, the pair smashed into the shrubbery where the stone gargoyle and entrance to the Zissuru Crypt. Regretting having destroyed the mechanism for the entrance, John delivered a solid uppercut and launched up and over the impressive hulk of The Ripper to land behind him on the damp mud. Preparing for another attack, John was jolted roughly against the ivy-covered wall as The Ripper slammed an elbow into his chest.

Giving John no time to recover, The Ripper effectively used John as a punchbag as he slammed his enormous fists into John's sides relentlessly. Disorientated by the flurry of blows, all John could do was curl his torso forward to lessen the impacts as The Ripper continued his onslaught. Acting out of pure desperation, John snatched for the baton and ripped it out in one swift movement. Caught by the momentum of his attacks, John dragged the baton down The Ripper's face leaving a jagged wound stretching from his eye to its mouth leaving a grotesque injury on his face.

'Bastard.'

Still reeling from the blows, John could not muster a retort as he pushed himself away from the wall and slammed his forearm into The Ripper's throat sending him collapsing backwards. Following through with the attack the pair crashed to the ground and John heard the hollow echo as they landed on top of the concealed entrance to the crypt. Pushing The Ripper into the ground, John manifested the same swirling smoke he had used on the Revenant on the rooftop and pushed it down into the ground. Burning through the grass, the pair felt the heavy stone above the entrance rumble and shake before finally giving way beneath them.

Dropping onto the winding staircase, the impact threw John from atop The Ripper and sent him rolling down the stone stairs. Coming to rest on the solid floor, he had time to look up as The Ripper came careering down towards him. Moving just in time, The Ripper came to rest where John had been laid and immediately the demon recognised his surroundings through his undamaged eye.

'You're not keeping me here.' the Ripper spat and turned to launch back up the stairs.

Still disorientated, John dragged the swirling smoke down towards The Ripper and blocked his way back up to the rainy surface. Fighting to keep the smoke in position, John watched as The Ripper placed his hand against it and recoiled with the sudden surge of pain.

'We are back here again, where you should have stayed in the first place.'

John launched the swirling smoke up towards the shattered opening to the crypt. Filling the opening, the crypt was once again sealed from the outside world. As John looked at The Ripper, he knew this was his last chance to trap the demon in the Zissuru. Preparing himself for the furious fight that was to follow, John shrugged off his control over the smoke barrier and waited for The Ripper to attack.

Carved from the stone beneath Hyde Park, the Zissuru was an almost perfect square. Moving around the bottom of the steps, the circle carved into the floor suddenly burst into flames as John teetered close to crossing the line. They both knew the area within the flaming circle marked the demon barrier that would, if The Ripper passed over the flaming lines, become its tomb. As the crypt was bathed in the curious blue light of the dancing flames, The Ripper attacked. Being sure to remain in the space between the wall and circle of shimmering flame, the fight between John and The Ripper was furious.

John knew there was desperation in The Ripper's attack. Being trapped within the Zissuru, the demon knew its fate was doomed unless it could release the smoking spell that now blocked his only means of escape. John knew The Ripper would stop at nothing to break free of the tomb and, like a trapped animal, The was now at his most dangerous. Willing to do anything for his survival, John blocked blow after blow, hoping to find a weakness in the relentless attacks that now flew at him from every direction.

Shielding his face from another clenched fist, John caught sight of something in the flickering light but recognised it too late. Dragging the hooked blade of a curious weapon through the air, terror overcame John as he recognised the crescent-shaped gold blade. Knowing the power of the Moon-Blade, John had no time to comprehend how The Ripper was in possession of it, but he knew that should either of the golden tips touch his lifeless heart, his existence would end. Jumping back, John felt the sting of pain as the blades connected with his chest, leaving two neat lines of smouldering flesh in their wake.

'She tells me everything.' The Ripper snarled as he lurched forward again with the Moon-Blade. 'Everything she doesn't even realise she knows.'

'Let her go!' John snapped as he jumped back to avoid another pair of smouldering scars across his chest. 'She's got nothing to do with this. It's me you want.'

'Seeing your care for her only makes me want to consume her soul all the more. It's just a shame you won't live to see it.

Driving the Moon-Blade at John's neck, John caught The Ripper's wrists but once again found himself pushed back against the solid wall of the stone crypt. Pushing back against The Ripper's tremendous strength, John's eyes were wide inside the plague doctor mask as the weapon pushed closer to his neck.

'I want to see the fear in your eyes.' The Ripper barked as he ripped the mask from John's face and tossed it into the flames.

Seeing the mask dissolve in the blue flames, John could feel the searing heat of the golden blade as it inched closer to his neck. Looking into the gaping wound that was left where The Ripper's eye had been, John knew he was trapped and under no illusion the sheer strength and size of The Ripper left him with no chance of escape.

'I'm not scared.' John lied.

'Oh, but you are. Not for yourself, but for her. Who is she to you?'

'Nobody. I just regret bringing her into this world and exposing her to you.'

Ripping his hand back, The Ripper broke free of John's grasp and held the Moon-Blade above his head, ready to strike. Accepting his fate, John closed his eyes and offered The Ripper one final quip.

'I absolve her soul of any connection to mine. End my existence and she will be free of me. Free from you.'

Knowing his sacrifice would protect Kimberley from The Ripper's grasp, John dropped his hands to his side and allowed the Ripper to deliver the final blow.

27

—·—

SEVERED CONNECTION

Having awoken in the bed, dazed and confused, Kimberley could not see when she had opened her eyes. To her, it felt only as if her eyelids were unwilling to open but, in truth, her eyes were open but shrouded in a milky haze. Her normally vibrant green eyes were nothing more than milky white, with only the faintest hint of colour underneath.

As the medical staff moved in a panic around her, Kimberley's apprehension, and fear grew. Unbeknownst to her, John and The Ripper were gone and Diana was nowhere to be seen. Time passed at an infuriatingly slow pace as the nurses drugged Kimberley back into a sedated slumber. Once again consumed by unconsciousness, there was something different this time.

Having been dragged back from her existence in The Ripper's memories, she had been close to finding her own way out when her view of Victorian London had disintegrated around her. At first she had panicked, having been consumed by the memory for so long. The thought of escaping had been all she had been concerned with, and yet now it had arrived, she was frightened. Struggling to remember where she had been before diving into the memory, Kimberley did not know where she would wake up.

Raking her fingers through the dust of the crumbling world, Kimberley had tasted her first mouthful of sterile air as the city was replaced by a blurred view of the hospital room. Through the milky glaze of her eyes, Kimberley had been able to sense movement but make out no detail of who, or what, was moving around her. Fighting to clear her vision, Kimberley's reaction had been entirely natural, but wild and dangerous. Feeling the prick of the needle, the sedatives worked quickly to suppress her violence and disorientation.

'You can't leave him.' The woman's voice hissed in the darkness.

Unable to see anything in her semi-conscious state, Kimberley looked around to find the source of the voice. It was not unfamiliar, it belonged to a woman from the memories who had seen and spoke to her without activating the ripples and turning the memories against her. Despite their contact, Kimberley did not know the woman's name, but somehow felt secure in her presence.

'Where are you?' Kimberley's voice trembled.

'I'm with you, but you need to be somewhere else.'

'What do you mean?'

'He needs you.'

'I don't even know where I am.'

Immediately, the world burst into view around her. Lit by candlelight, Kimberley shielded her eyes from the sudden glare and allowed the flickering flames to settle before she removed her hand from her face. Allowing her eyes to adjust, Kimberley now stood in a vast graveyard, surrounded by headstones and statues of angels. Having no recollection of a place like this, Kimberley searched for the source of the voice and saw the woman's familiar silhouette in the next row of headstones.

'Where are we?'

'We are at the end.' The woman declared and turned to face her.

Stopping in her tracks, Kimberley did not recognise the face that looked at her. The last tie they had met, the woman had been in her thirties, youthful and kind, and now it was an old woman that greeted her. Taken aback, Kimberley composed herself and inched closer, keeping enough space between the two of them in case this was another trick of the memories she now inhabited.

'What happened to you?'

'Life, life happened to me.' The old woman smiled, the creases in her face deepening as she did. 'But now my time has come to join my husband and say goodbye to the world.'

'Why have you helped me? Why are you different from all the others in here?'

'Because I am not the same as these things. I am here to show you a way out, to guide you to your freedom whereas the others are here to imprison you.'

'That doesn't answer why!'

'Because *he* asked me to.'

Pointing her shaking finger to the gravestone in front of her, Kimberley moved closer to inspect the etched stone. Encased in ivy, she had no choice but to drop to her knees and pull the creeping vines away from the weathered stone face of the headstone. Even without seeing the name, Kimberley knew who it belonged to. Pulling a large clump of vegetation from the stone, she was greeted with the name she had expected to see:

JOHN BARTRAM SMITH
BELOVED FATHER AND HUSBAND

Stepping back from the gravestone, Kimberley turned her attention to the elderly woman who stood beside her.

'You are his only hope.'

'I only met him a few days ago.'

'A lot can happen in such a short space of time, my dear.' The old woman moved closer and placed her quivering hand on Kimberley's cheek.

Looking into the old woman's eyes, Kimberley could see movement in their depths. As the old woman inched closer, she felt drawn into the dark pupils, needing to see what flickered and danced behind them.

'I don't even know where I am, so how am I supposed to help him?'

'Follow his heart.'

'What does that mean?' Kimberley snapped, wanting to pull back but feeling hypnotised by the curious movement behind the woman's eyes.

'I am his heart.' The woman declared. 'He has left me here to guide you to him. Your time is now, as is his.'

With their noses almost touching, Kimberley dared not move as the old woman held her gaze. In the depths of her eyes, Kimberley could make out movement, frantic and frenzied, but lacking enough detail to see exactly what was happening. Desperate to find out what was happening, Kimberley heard the woman's hushed words before the old woman decayed before her very eyes.

'You are connected to both of them. Do what you can to save John.'

The old woman's skin turned pale and Kimberley backed away. The woman staggered back and fell into the now open grave beside John's. By the time Kimberley had taken the half-dozen steps to the open graveside, all that remained in the deep hole was the skinless skeleton of the old woman, long ago dead.

'How do I do that then?' Kimberley screamed in frustration and turned away from the disturbing things within the open grave.

The sight behind her was not what she expected. The grave-yard no long stretched out in front of her and instead she stood in Hyde Park, moments after John and The Ripper had disap-peared into the Zissuru crypt. Unsure if she was back from the memories of the past, she inched closer to the jagged hole in the ground and caught sight of the same movement she had seen in the eyes of the dying old woman.

With no care for the consequences, Kimberley launched down the steps and immediately saw the two men fighting beside the roaring wall of shimmering blue fire. Seeing The Ripper drag the Moon-Blade across The Raven's chest, Kimberley realised she was mimicking every movement of The Ripper. Holding her hand in the air behind her head, she knew what was to come as, with her empty hand, she reached out and copied the same movements as The Ripper tore the plague doctor mask from John's face.

It was then, in that single moment, as John watched the flames consume the mask, that their gazes met. Even though Kimberley could not be sure she was even present in that moment, something about the look on John's face told her he had seen her. Still holding her hand high above her head, Kimberley knew the attack would follow and watched with frustration as John appeared to give up.

Lowering his defences, dropping both arms to his side, she could only watch in disbelief as John closed his eyes.

'What are you doing?' Kimberley tried to scream, but her voice was soundless.

Feeling her hand move forward, she realised The Ripper was about to deliver his ultimate blow. Punching the Moon-Blade towards John's chest, Kimberley fought to keep her own hand from moving, but felt she had no control over her own body.

All she could do was silently scream as she desperately longed to stop her arm from moving.

At last, her voice pierced the eerie silence of the crypt. Barely above a whisper at first, her defiant scream reached a crescendo and The Ripper's attack hung frozen in mid-air. Seeing his face contort with frustration, Kimberley fought with every ounce of strength to keep The Ripper's attack from finding its mark.

'Do something!' Kimberley yelped in terror as her clenched fist inched further forward despite her effort to control it.

John had seen Kimberley and in doing so, had trusted himself to her. His fate was sealed without her. He knew that. Having surrendered himself to his end, it had been enough of a distraction to keep The Ripper from realising Kimberley had joined them in the Zissuru. Seeing the look of victorious satisfaction on his opponent's face, John had closed his eyes and waited for fate to decide.

Hearing Kimberley's defiant scream, he opened his eyes and saw the look of terror on The Ripper's face as the Moon-Blade hung frozen in the air by the side of his head. Stall trapped against the wall, John could sense the frustration as The Ripper willed his shaking hand to obey his command and deliver his final blow.

'Do something!'

Desperation laced her words as Kimberley fought to keep control of The Ripper for as long as she could. Not wanting to waste the distraction, John reached up and prised the Moon-Blade from The Ripper's vice-like grip.

'How?' Was all the frenzied demon could muster as John snatched the blade free.

'Sometimes, fate gifts us an ally. Something you wouldn't know anything about.'

Dragging the Moon-Blade down, John severed The Ripper's hand, allowing him to drop to the ground. Kicking the severed hand into the flames, the only part of The Ripper that could move was his remaining eye. Still fighting to break free of whatever magic connected him to Kimberley, The Ripper roared in frustration, but it was too late. Fighting to move his body, John wasted no time and used the Moon-Blade to his advantage.

Wielding the weapon, John scooped the curved blade through the air and despite everything, The Ripper caught the attack in his uninjured hand. Shrugging free of Kimberley's connection, The Ripper glared at John over the curved Moon-Blade. Still crouched, John was once again at a disadvantage as The Ripper's muscular frame loomed over him.

'You're nothing but a pawn in a much larger game.' The Ripper spat. 'You don't deserve the power of Death's Hand. You should have died that night.'

'I did.' John snarled through gritted teeth. 'And because of it, you made me into this.'

Pressing up with every ounce of strength, John fought against The Ripper's grip and drove the Moon-Blade upwards. With one last push, John shifted his weight, breaking free of The Ripper and span the blade through the air. His movement was impossibly fast and before The Ripper knew what had happened, John was once again poised and ready for a follow up attack.

There was no need for anything more from John. In the seconds following the strike, The Ripper didn't move. Instead, the muscular creature blinked once before his head toppled from his shoulders. As the head came to rest at John's feet, he delivered the final blow and sank the Moon-Blade into The Ripper's chest and pushed him back through the wall of blue flame and into the demon circle.

Driving through the wall of flame, John landed atop the headless hulk as he ripped his hand out of the gaping wound in The Ripper's chest. Hooking the blade to his back, where the escrima stick had once sat, John could see the lifeless heart in The Ripper's chest. Taking hold of the blackened heart, John tore it free of the chest and watched as the lifeless flesh turned to crimson crystal in his hand. Knowing The Ripper was done, John dropped the heart and let it rest on The Ripper's torso as its body turned to ash and the wall of fire dissipated back into the ground.

'Is he dead?' Kimberley quizzed from across the room.

'He was never really alive.' John replied as he turned to look at her. 'Where are you?'

'I thought I was here, with you?'

'Only your spirit.' John answered as he looked around the crypt. 'I'll come and find you. Just wait for my voice.'

Before he could say anything else, Kimberley faded away, leaving him alone in the Zissuru crypt. Taking one last look at the crystal heart that now lay on the stone floor, John was overcome with relief that he had once again succeeded in ending The Ripper's reign of terror. Seeing the dead heart on the ground, John knew he had done more this time. Whereas before he had used the enchantments of the Zissuru crypt to trap The Ripper for eternity, this time he had banished him from existence.

'There's no coming back from that one, Jack.' John smirked as he moved towards the stairs. 'Maybe now I can get some bloody rest.'

Feeling the aches and pains from his battle with The Ripper, John took a moment before leaving the Zissuru crypt for the last time, he hoped.

28

—·—

OUT OF THE DARKNESS

'She'll be fine. Bring her around.'

'I'm not sure that's wise.'

'I'll take responsibility for her.'

The room fell silent, and at last everything changed.

John was sitting beside Kimberley's hospital bed, accompanied by three nurses and a very concerned looking doctor. They all watched as one nurse injected a small amount of fluid into Kimberley's drip and took a hasty step away from the bed.

'She was violent last time,' the doctor pleaded. 'That's why we sedated her. You should prepare yourself.'

'I'm fine. You can leave us.'

'But...'

John ended the conversation with a stern look and, without hesitation, the doctor and nurses left him alone in the room. Closing the door behind them, John waited by Kimberley's side as the drugs took their effect and the sleepiness wore off. Seeing her eyes moving beneath her eyelids, John somehow found himself poised and waiting with a nervous anticipation. Seeing

Kimberley's pale skin, he still felt a tremendous amount of guilt at the trauma he had put her through and yet, without her, he most likely would not be where he was.

'Do you have to be so loud?'

'I haven't said anything.' John offered as Kimberley opened her eyes. 'Want me to sit you up?'

'Please.'

Finding the controls for the bed, John raised Kimberley as she took a moment to collect herself. With the bed upright, John sat back in his chair and waited for Kimberley to speak.

'Are you just going to sit there and not say anything?' Kimberley coughed as she took a sip of water.

'It's difficult to say anything, all things considered.'

'In the short time I've known you, that's not something that I'm used to.' She offered a forced smile to disguise her discomfort. 'It's hard to know what was real.'

'There's one thing I need to say before we talk about what happened.'

'What's that?'

'Thank you.' John's words hung in the air for a moment, tangible to both of them. 'If you hadn't helped me in the crypt, The Ripper would have ended me.'

'I don't even know how I got there.'

John watched as Kimberley took a moment to move through the blurred, shared memories that filled her head. Knowing the turbulent thoughts that would be racing through her mind,

John gave her time to compose herself and moved to the window.

'I'm glad they moved you rooms.' John remarked as he admired the original window frame. 'I expect we left something of a mess behind us.'

'You were here?'

'Both of us were. It was you that brought us together, the fact he infected your mind and fed from your knowledge to seek me out.'

'I don't know anything about you.' Kimberley protested. 'I only know what you've shown me, and that's not a lot when you think of who and what you are!'

'You know more than you realise.' John sighed as he rested his hands on the windowsill and looked at the lights illuminating the Houses of Parliament. 'By giving you access to my memories, I gave you access to everything. While you were consciously aware of things, your mind has a connection to everything I cannot consciously control.'

'It sounds so messy, and it's the reason I was locked in there, isn't it?'

'Yes. You were the conduit for both of us, that's what made your escape impossible.' John was lost in his thoughts for a moment, before he continued. 'I think The Ripper knew just how much to let you roam, enough to feed him what he needed and yet enough to keep you on a tight leash.'

'I'm done with this.' Kimberley suddenly declared. 'Whatever it is you've got me into, I'm done.'

John turned to look at the young woman sat up in the hospital bed. There could be no denying her logic. She had seen more in the few days since they had first met in the Nuthall Hospital, than she had in her entire life. He could see her deep scars when he looked at her.

'Some injuries appear easier to accept when you can see them.' John offered as he moved back to the foot of her bed. 'Others that sit inside are much more difficult for people to understand or even accept. With nothing tangible, they will always doubt the severity of things.'

'It feels like I've lived in a nightmare.'

'You have.' There was sorrow and regret in John's voice. 'I did not know what I was dragging you into, and I'm sorry. I never intended to take you this deep and I know all too well the scars you now carry.'

'If this is what I am left feeling after just a few days, what must it be like for you?'

John fumbled to find an answer. Feeling Kimberley's gaze, he tried to lighten his answer with a feigned smile, but it soon faded with Kimberley's stern gaze in response. Dropping to perch on the end of the hospital bed, John took a moment to find the right words to give her an answer. Realising he had never spoken to anyone else about the dark world he occupied, finding the right way to explain it suddenly felt like an impossible task. Taking a deep breath, John looked to the ceiling and, for the first time in decades, felt *emotion*.

'It's a fate I accepted a long time ago, but that doesn't mean it's easy. I always wondered why Azrael never released me from my oath when I banished The Ripper into the Zissuru crypt all those years ago, and now I know why. My job wasn't done.' Almost absent-mindedly, John toyed with the pale bedsheets as he spoke. 'Having done this for so long, I suppose I've boxed away the darkness and hold away the feelings that come with what I see and experience.'

'That isn't particularly healthy.'

'What's healthy for a dead guy?' John quipped with a raised eyebrow and despite herself, Kimberley chuckled. 'But I know you're right. I've always pushed on through, locking each piece of the damaged puzzle away in another box and pretending it's not mine.'

'They call it disassociation,' Kimberley added. 'It's a very common defence mechanism, but it doesn't come without its own issues.'

'It's probably best I leave you to your recovery. Even if the doctors can't understand why, your vitals will convince them to keep you here until you're strong enough to go home.'

John made to rise from the bed and stopped when he felt Kimberley's soft hand on top of his. Frozen by the sudden sensation somewhere in the pit of his stomach, he turned to look and found her propped up, leaning close to him so she could whisper in his ear. Even though she knew they were alone, what she wanted to say needed to be something between just the two of them.

'Even the little of what I've seen, I can't imagine the pain you must feel.'

'I don't have feelings anymore, not really.'

'They're in there, I see the look in your eyes.' Kimberley placed her hand over where his lifeless heart sat in his chest. 'You have my gratitude, and sympathy, for what you've lost over the years and I pray you'll one day find peace.'

'One day.' John choked.

'While I'm saying this is the end of my journey with you, you always know where you can find me. Even the dead sometimes need to talk.'

Kimberley offered a smile and John fought back the surge of emotions he had long bottled away and suppressed to the back of his mind. Looking into the eyes of the young woman, John knew their journey together was over. Although she made the offer, they both knew he would not accept. If there was one emotion, one feeling, they both knew he could feel, it was guilt, and he had a tremendous amount about what he had put Kimberley through.

Leaning across, John kissed her on the forehead as a father would kiss a daughter.

'I wish you the best of life, Kimberley Mansfield.' John rose from the bed. 'I'll always keep one beady eye on you, my dear.'

'What will you do now?'

'I expect I'll make sense of the mess. There's Revenants bouncing around out there, and judging by the warden's decision to call for help from the Society, I expect my sanctuary as a broken mind in the Nuthall has long lost its safety.'

'Take care, John Smith.'

'You can call me The Raven.' Manifesting the plague doctor mask over his face, John waited a second before disappearing from the hospital room, leaving Kimberley alone.

Putting as much space as he could between St Thomas' and himself, John found his perch atop the spires of Tower Bridge once again. Having exposed himself to the living in the hospital room, John ensured his presence was once again shrouded from the blind masses below. Balancing on the steel crossbeams of the bridge, John watched London's hustle and bustle around him.

Unwilling to remove the mask, John allowed a solitary tear to roll down his cheek inside the leather. Unseen by anyone, John's sadness was not only for Kimberley but also the memories he had with the hospital. So much of his life had been centred on that place and the irony it had been where Kimberley had been taken was not lost on him. Allowing the short-lived emotion to run its course, John simply watched the world moving below.

Hearing the heavy toll of Big Ben travelling along the Thames, John knew there was no point in asking for Death's guidance. He knew he was, as ever, alone on this journey.

'Maybe it's better this way.' Azrael offered as he appeared on the bridge behind him. 'Death's Hand is a lonely duty.'

'Will she be free of it, or have I cursed her to a life filled with the evil we fight to keep at bay?'

'She will move on,' Azrael comforted as he moved to join John on the crossbeam. 'If you let her.'

'Am I done?'

'Not yet. There's more for you to do.'

'There always is!' John groaned as he admired the sunlight shimmering off the glass of the distant skyscrapers.

'For what it's worth, I'm proud of what you did.'

'Thanks.'

Silence descended between the pair of them. As they both drank in the majestic view from atop Tower Bridge, there was nothing that needed to be said. The Raven's duties remained unfulfilled. There were demons to be found and order to be restored. But, all things considered, they both knew he needed a moment. Instead of marching blindly into his next confrontation with evil, John needed a moment to remember what this was all for.

London was alive and although they were blind to their need, the world needed people like John to protect them.

As The Raven, he remained Death's Hand.

A forgotten sentinel.

Recruited by Death.

To protect us from evil.

29

— • —

CHESS PIECES

D iana looked at the now shrouded side of the Old Police Station. Police tape had marked off the area around the side of the cell block and a large tent placed over the entrance to the crypt. Taking a moment to admire Hyde Park now the weather had lifted, she waited for Qamar to finish speaking to the senior detective by the side of the large tent. Taking her cue from a subtle wave of Qamar's hand, she walked over, carrying herself with an air or confidence and authority.

'Damien here has agreed to allow us access.' Qamar declared as he lifted the scene tape to allow Diana access. 'As long as we don't disturb anything.'

'Make it quick.' The detective snapped as Qamar shook his hand. 'I'm risking a lot letting you in there.'

'Brother,' Qamar offered with a knowing smile as he pulled his hand back. 'Our presence will be no louder than the whispers of our existence.'

'Good.'

Clearly frustrated by the situation, the grumpy detective stalked back towards the Old Police Station frontage. Once they were alone, save for the pair of community support officers on the far end of the tape, they found the entrance to the tent and stepped in.

'I am disappointed we didn't destroy this place.' Diana remarked as she stepped through the jagged entrance hole and descended the steps.

'What good would that have been?' Qamar quizzed as he followed behind. 'It has served its purpose to perfection.'

Grateful to find the crypt illuminated by portable lights, they made their way with ease down the sweeping stone staircase. Upon reaching the bottom, both Diana and Qamar took a moment to admire their surroundings. Bathed in the artificial light, they could see the symbols and emblems carved into the stone walls and ceiling. Seeing the deep etched lines of the protective circle, Diana was careful to step over as she moved into the room's centre.

'Such a waste.' Diana hushed as she moved to the only remnant of The Ripper in the centre of the circle.

Despite the charred outline on the ground showing where The Ripper had been, only his heart remained on the ground. Appearing as a human heart, the crystal surface reflected light in all directions as Diana waved her hand in front of the crystal heart. Not daring to touch the sacred remnants of the demon, she admired the curious beauty of the heart.

'A necessary waste though, wouldn't you agree?'

'Oh yes, indeed.' Diana beamed as she rose from her haunches. 'While I would have liked to see The Ripper grow into something more, I expect this was his inevitable end.'

Stalking around the length and breadth of the crypt, Diana traced her fingers across the various symbols covering the wall.

'You've got to admit, there is something about this place. You can almost feel the power in the air.'

'Have we heard anything of where he's gone?'

'The Raven? Nothing yet.'

'The police cannot give me anything.'

'What are we doing about the witnesses?' Diana quizzed, as she admired one particular carving on the wall that depicted a twisted demon's face taller than her. 'Have they been silenced?'

'The media have been controlled.' Qamar offered as he too took the time to admire the red crystal heart on the ground. 'We have explained the damage as a failed terror attack, something about dissidents and a prisoner they wanted to break free. It will be enough to appease the masses who crave nothing more than excitement to maintain their ignorance to the real world.'

'And the witnesses?'

'Rest easy Diana, we have silenced them where necessary.'

'Good.' There was a coldness to her reply, something that was not lost on Qamar. 'I would hate for these events to stir attention when we need to operate in the shadows now more than ever.'

'Do you believe the prophecy will be fulfilled?'

'With what has come to pass within these very walls?' Yes.'
Diana paused before turning to face Qamar, the enormous
carved demon dominating the wall behind her. 'The fire in his
heart has been reignited. The John Smith that sat as nothing but
a shell of his former self has shed his skin, and The Raven has
been reborn.'

'And the girl?'

'She has played her part to perfection, as I knew she would.'
Diana replied with a devilish grin. We have manipulated and
maneuvered John Smith into position.

'Then the preparations will begin.'

'First we must find him.' Diana corrected as she moved back
towards the stairs. 'Empowered as he is, he will be harder to
find.'

'Not for the Revenants.' Qamar declared and in response,
three of the Revenants appeared in the crypt behind him as if
summoned by his words. 'With his reconnection to his power
as Death's Hand, it will make him easier for them to find him.'

'We will not fail you.' The lead Revenant declared.

'Pray you don't.' Diana snapped. 'Your predecessor faced our
wrath for his failure. Succeed or suffer the same fate.'

Not offering anything else, Diana and Qamar left the three
Revenants alone in the crypt. From the outside, nobody would
know what had just happened or what had manifested in the
derelict subterranean tomb. Chattering their teeth together,
seeking any signs of The Raven, the trio of demonic hunters
shared a common purpose.

To find The Raven and bring him into the fold of the Full Moon Society.

— • —

The Raven was born from a long-standing idea that finally found a home as a screenplay. Developed initially as a TV Pilot, "Origins" is currently under consideration for adaptation to the silver screen. Designed to reflect a limited run or multi-season series, the adventures and journey of *The Raven* will reflect an episodic process with a number of novellas representing each individual "episode" as it were.

You can find out more about the future of *The Raven* at **WWW.TOBEY-ALEXANDER.COM/RAVEN** where you can also see some exclusive concept artwork that accompanies the pitch and series bibles delivered to studio executives for their consideration.

There is more to come with the final three "episodes" in the sequel book...

https://books2read.com/TheRaven4-6

books2read.com/TheRaven4-6

Bonus Artwork

What follows are some early concept sketches for scenes within the book. See if you can't picture these moments in the story you've just enjoyed.

Kimberley Mansfield's part in the chess-game of John's return
to his position as The Raven cannot be understated. Very much
ignorant to the world she is about to encounter, Kimberley is
quick to dismiss John's stories and stories from a broken mind.

We see her here as a busy graduate with only her thesis on
her mind. WHat she doesn't know is her encounter with John
Smith will forever change her future and her understanding of
the world.

A natural reaction to her exploration of John's past is to *run*. The terror of what she has encountered is expressed here in a simple yet compelling view of her turning from John and fleeing in terror. Such a simple interaction becomes the foundation of a new experience and understanding of the world.

The Raven's birth is an aspect of the story that means so much.
Not only do we need to know the Raven's source and birth,
but how he stands as a broken emblem of what he once was.
The Raven's birth from Death is shown here in an image that
captures the strength and power of a man becoming, something
more.

The look on Kimberley's face here is important to show her acceptance of what she has done. By now you have seen her part and the willingness in which she stepped into this new world. Even in the three images of her contained here, we see an evolution of strength and resolve in a character from such a simple interaction.

The Raven in Origins is a curious dichotomy, we see the power of his creation but we also see him in the modern world disconnected and somewhat broken from his oath. With Origins, the essence of the Raven's evolution is one of *potential*.

We see Death (Azrael) as he stalks the Victorian streets in search of Death's Hand. Ever in the background, Azrael is an essence that lingers in the shadows, a silent supporter of John's journey to becoming The Raven.

John, as The Raven, shares a moment with Kimberley after meeting the Revenant on the London rooftops. We can see John's feelings of responsibility and how Kimberley has, by virtue of their paths crossing, become his ward. This connection and its consequences weigh heavily on John through the story.

Even without the shroud of The Raven, John struggles to find his place in modern London. Awash with echoes of the past, John fights on all levels to find his purpose and powers after so long.